JEANNE HYVRARD:
WATERWEED
IN THE WASH-HOUSES

Also published by Edinburgh University Press

The Dead Girl in a Lace Dress
by Jeanne Hyvrard
Jeanne Hyvrard: Theorist of the Modern World
by Jennifer Waelti-Walters

JEANNE HYVRARD:
WATERWEED
IN THE WASH-HOUSES

Translated by
Elsa Copeland

EDINBURGH UNIVERSITY PRESS

La Meurtritude © 1977 by Les Éditions de Minuit, Paris

Translation © 1996 Elsa Copeland

Introduction © 1996 Jennifer Waelti-Walters

Edinburgh University Press Ltd
22 George Square
Edinburgh EH8 9LF

Typeset in Caslon
by Pioneer Associates, Perthshire, and
printed and bound in Great Britain

A CIP record for this book is available from
the British Library

ISBN 0 7486 0822 2

CONTENTS

INTRODUCTION

Jeanne Hyvrard, a Parisian writer born in 1945, who has lived and travelled extensively in the Third World, began to be published in 1975. *Waterweed in the Wash-houses* (*La Meurtritude*, 1977) is her third novel. She is a teacher of political economy in a technical high school in Paris, is married to a fellow economist and has one daughter who is an engineer.

In the twenty years that Hyvrard has been writing, she has consistently proved herself to be one of the most exciting thinkers and innovative stylists writing in France, though she has not yet received the public recognition given to some of her contemporaries, Hélène Cixous and Luce Irigaray for example, with whom she has much in common both in her way of writing and in her understanding of the female condition. Her major theme is chaos in the world today. This chaos has a philosophical and theological root in the biblical description of Creation, political manifestations in the post-colonial upheavals of our time, and a literary presence as metaphor in her work. And it is clearly a thought process parallel to that which has produced scientific chaos theory.[1]

Hyvrard is a visionary and a prophet, a poet and an economist. She translates into her work knowledge that she has acquired from a myriad sources and which makes dis-orderly sense, profound and chaotic sense at a stage of pre-consciousness where it cannot yet be reduced to purely rational terms. Not for nothing does she begin to write every day at three or four in the morning, still close to the realms of dream, for her writing is richly evocative and metaphorical (in some ways reminiscent of the writing of women in the Surrealist movement), while showing precise awareness of the levels of oppression in our post-colonial economic system.

Her first book, *Les Prunes de Cythère* (The Plums of Cythera, 1975), is, Hyvrard maintains to this day, a report on the economic conditions of Martinique. It is also a dense and multifaceted exploration, within language, of the situation of the oppressed and the marginalised: women and colonised peoples in particular. Language and its capacities for expression are intrinsic to Hyvrard's quest and she is constantly forcing the French language to exceed its grammatically and culturally imposed limits in order to create a vehicle for her 'fusional' thought – that is, thinking contrary aspects together within a shifting network of connections. This is Chaos in its original form as the face against which the logos sets itself.

Her next book, *Mère la mort* (Mother Death, 1976),[2] focuses on women's historic deprivation of a language, a culture and a traditional spirituality. It also shows the scapegoating of women judged mad within the logarchical system - that is, Western thought since the Enlighten-ment with its insistence on reason to the exclusion of all other forms of understanding.

Next, published together as twin texts, are *Les Doigts du*

figuier and *La Meurtritude* (1977).[3] ('Waterweed in the Wash-houses' was Hyvrard's own original title, to which the translator chose to return.) The novel begins with the story of Creation as told in the Bible. Hyvrard uses André Chouraqui's translation into French as her starting point,[4] then transposes and re-encodes the first thirty-four verses of Genesis to create an abstract system out of the concrete terms of her original. Thus 'Elohim created the heavens and the earth' becomes 'The spirit conceived of negations and affirmation'; 'And it is the evening and the morning: third day' becomes 'And it is union and separation: third differentiation'.

Hyvrard constructs for her readers a perspective on the world in terms of separation and fusion, chaos and logos which provides a specific context for the words that recur frequently in her novel. In a sense, like a mathematician, she writes the theorem first and then proceeds to apply it. If this seems off-putting, readers who are more comfortable with the stream-of-consciousness narration of the rest of the book can just skip the opening and come back to it later to see whether it then makes sense to them. The key words of the code are separation, fusion, contrary, negation and chaotic. They refer to our learned preference for rationality and our linguistic and mental habits of separation and categorisation begun, in Judaeo-Christianity, when God gave Adam the right to name all creatures, thus differentiating them one from the other.

Hyvrard believes that reason has its place but that it provides a restricted, constricting and linear perspective on a world where everything is interconnected and where it is necessary to acknowledge the 'chaos' and think things together – fusional thought. In her later work this will bring her to considerations ever more analogous to chaos theory, and anyone familiar with the workings of chaos and the patterning of fractal geometry will find similar structures in Hyvrard's style even here in her early work.

At this point she is struggling to find a way of writing within the logical, grammatical structures of the French language which will enable her to create networks of connection, metaphoric reverberations, that express the complexities, paradoxes and constant motion inherent in an understanding of the human condition in its lived reality rather than according to the explanatory structures that Western cultures have been constructing since the Renaissance.

Here some of the major metaphoric links she establishes are on the one hand: light and enlightenment, Adam and reason, male and analysis; and on the other: darkness and fusion, night and confusion, waters and contrariness (not opposites), seas and 'contrarations' (when the word she needs is missing from the language, she invents it), female and synthesis. Some of these are juxtapositions that are customary in the binary oppositional system we use frequently: male-female, analysis-synthesis, for example. The shift in Hyvrard's writing is that she refuses to set these contrary notions in opposition to each other so that one negates the other but insists, rather, on the connection between them as two aspects of one thought.

It is not easy to maintain such a thought process in a language and tradition of definition, dictionaries, tax-onomies and hierarchies of importance. When she wrote *La Meurtritude* Hyvrard was searching for a linguistic and metaphorical structure to express the interconnections. She had tried chess in *Mère la mort*, but chess is both binary and oppositional and proved unsatisfactory. The French word for checkmate is 'mat', and 'Mat' is also the name for the Fool in the Tarot cards. Whether this was Hyvrard's point of connection or not, she chose as structuring metaphors for *La Meurtritude* the Tarot and alchemy because both are transformative systems and in each the constituent elements only have meaning in relation to each other in an ever-changing context.

In Tarot the cards must be shuffled and laid out to provide a reading. In alchemy lead is transmuted into gold through a series of transformations, transformations which occur on three distinct yet inter-related planes: the laboratory where the physical changes occur; literature, where the metamorphoses are expressed in terms of the activities of the gods (Mercury=mercury, Venus=copper, and so on); and the soul of the alchemist. If the alchemist's spiritual process towards perfection is impaired then the experiment will abort, because the underlying belief is that the alchemist is attempting a symbolic imitation of the seven days of Creation and, in so doing, becomes an 'ape of God', attempting ever greater proximity to divinity and perfection. Each system is in constant motion across and through time. They appear to be fragments of a lost language and, as such, very appropriate vehicles for Hyvrard's thought as she moves towards a satisfactory style of her own.

The two systems together provide both the narrative structure and characters of the novel (the Major Arcana: Emperor, Empress, Lovers *et al*) and a frame for the mental transmutations of the narrator from stage to stage, 'death' to 'death'.

Jeanne, the narrator, as in the previous novels, is considered mad because she refuses to conform to what is accepted by those around her as rational behaviour. She is searching for a sense of self, for her past, the lost heritage of all women, and a language in which to express the complexities of her interconnected understanding. The trees of the Garden of Eden, present in the earlier books, remain a central image in this exploration. The tree of knowledge and the tree of life give way here to a third tree: the murderer's tree – Cain's tree – which shrivels to become the tree of those murdered, the withered tree in alchemical symbolism, and ultimately the Cross of the Crucifixion. In yet another transformation, in *Les Doigts du figuier*, it becomes the fig-tree cursed by Jesus because it had no fruit.

In *Les Doigts du figuier* Hyvrard juxtaposes the fig and the grape, the lost goddess and (by implication) the Christian god who imprisoned her in the wine-press. This book-length narrative poem is an exploration of women's ways of being and knowing, women's bodies, and women's realities within a context of deliberate suppression and oppression.

After the first four books, Hyvrard became more clearly political and philosophical and as a result has been obliged to change publishers several times. (French publishers are not comfortable with women claiming public, political voices.) She has published two long prose texts concerning colonisation and post-colonisation, three long poems, all political but in different modes,[5] a book on cancer and its social institutions, and a philosophical dictionary in which she defines her terms and creates a textbook of the cross-referencing system of social criticism she uses in all her texts. The latest published volume is a semi-autobiographical novel: *La Jeune morte en robe de dentelle* (1990; *The Dead Girl in a Lace Dress*) which I and my colleague Jean-Pierre Mentha have translated and which is published at the same time as *Waterweed in the Wash-houses*. Hyvrard's most recent book, *Ton nom de végétal* (Your vegetable name), is due to be published by Editions Trois in Montreal. *Waterweed* is an early stage of an ever more challenging literary and philosophical odyssey.

Elsa Copeland, the translator of *La Meurtritude*, gave what turned out to be the last three years of her life to this work. She died in August 1993. A nun who taught French at Loyola University in Chicago, she encountered *La Meurtritude* in a summer school on contemporary women's writing taught by Germaine Brée. The text touched her deeply and, without any other knowledge of Hyvrard or her work, she undertook this very difficult piece of translation. Jeanne Hyvrard directed her to me. I am extremely grateful that I met Elsa, first through her delightful letters and then in person, and that I was able to get to know her a little through our mutual interest in this novel. This is the introduction I promised her I would write, and I do it in her memory. It is particularly poignant that Jeanne Hyvrard should have dedicated this novel 'to a dead woman'.

Jennifer Waelti-Walters
Victoria, B.C.
June 1995

NOTES

1 James Gleick, *Chaos: Making a New Science* (New York: Penguin Books, 1987).

2 *Mère la mort* (Paris: Les Editions de Minuit, 1975), translated as *Mother Death* by Laurie Edson (Lincoln: University of Nebraska Press, 1988).

3 *Les Doigts du figuier* (Paris: Les Editions de Minuit, 1977), translated as *The Fingers of the Fig-tree* by Helen Frances as part of her MA thesis, Victoria University of Wellington, New Zealand, 1987. Extracts from *La Meurtritude* (Paris: Les Editions de Minuit, 1977) were published in E. Fallaize (ed.), *French Women's Writing* (London: Macmillan, 1993).

4 André Chouraqui, trans., *La Bible: Entête* (Genesis) (Paris: Desclée de Brouwer, 1974).

5 Hyvrard's long poem *Que se partagent encore les eaux* was published with *La Baisure* by Des Femmes in 1985. There is an unpublished translation of *Que se partagent*, 'Let the waters part again', by Erica Grundman.

I

1 In the beginning the spirit conceived negations and affirmation.
2 Affirmation was chaotic, bottomless fusion, the breath of the spirit brooding over opposites.

3 The spirit says: 'Light will be'. And light is.
4 The spirit sees the light, that it is good. And the spirit separates the light from fusion.
5 The spirit calls the light 'Differentiation'. The fusion, he calls 'Confusion'.

It is both union and separation: unique differentiation.

6 The spirit says: 'A dividing line will be at the heart of opposites. It will be separant between opposites and opposites.'
7 The spirit creates the dividing line. He separates the opposites below the dividing line from the opposites above the dividing line. And so it is.
8 The spirit calls the dividing line: 'Negations'.

It is both union and separation: second differentiation.

9 The spirit says: 'Opposites will come together under negations toward a unique place and the thinkable will appear.' And so it is.
10 The spirit calls the thinkable: 'Affirmation'. The coming together of opposites, he calls: 'Contrarations'. The spirit sees that this is good.

11 The spirit says: 'Affirmation impels impulsion, instinct fertilising fertility, cognition bearing its fruits on its behalf, being fertile in affirmation.' And so it is.

12 Affirmation urges impulsion, instinct fertilising fertility on its behalf and knowledge bearing its fruits, being fertile on its behalf. The spirit sees that this is good.

13 And this is both union and separation: third differentiation.

14 The spirit says: 'There will be rules at the dividing line of negations to separate differentiation and confusion. They will be for the conjunctions and the reflections and the differentiations and the diversifications.

15 'They will be the rules for the dividing line of negations to illuminate affirmation.' And so it is.

16 The spirit makes two great rules: the great rule to dominate differentiation, the lesser rule to dominate confusion and memories.

17 The spirit gives them to the dividing line of negations to illuminate affirmation, to dominate differentiation and confusion, to separate the brightness from fusion. The spirit sees that this is good.

*

19 And this is both union and separation: fourth differentiation.

20 The spirit says: 'Opposites will abound, swarming with fruitful, confirming ideas, contradiction will hover over affirmation at the dividing line of negations.'

21 The spirit creates phantasms, fruitful confirming ideas that abound in opposites on their behalf and every contradiction contradicting on its behalf. The spirit sees that this is good.

22 The spirit praised them saying: 'Bear your fruits, abound, fill up opposites with contrarations and contradiction that they may abound over affirmation.

23 And this is both union and separation: fifth differentiation.

24 The spirit says: 'Affirmation will pursue the fruitful idea on its behalf, intuition, confirmation, the fruitfulness of the affirmation on its behalf.' And so it is.

25 The spirit makes the fruitfulness of the affirmation on its behalf, intuition on its behalf and every confirmation of the declaration on its behalf. The spirit sees that it is good.

26 The spirit says: 'We will make reasoning according to our shape, to our likeness. It will dominate the interrogation of opposites, the contradiction of negations, intuition, every affirmation, every confirmation which confirms the affirmation.'

27 The spirit conceives reasoning according to his shape, in the shape of spirit he conceives it. Analytical and synthetical he conceives them.

28 The spirit praises them. The spirit tells them: 'Bear your fruit, abound, fill up affirmation, conquer it, to dominate the interrogation of contraration, the contradiction of negations, all fruitfulness which confirms affirmation.'

29 The spirit says: 'Here now, I give you every instinct fertilising fertility over the full extent of all affirmation, and all knowledge which bears in itself the knowledge fertilising fertility: for you, this is your nourishment.

30 'For all fruitfulness of affirmation, for every contradiction of negations, for every confirmation of affirmation containing in itself the fruitful idea, every instinctive impulse is nourishment.' And so it is.

31 The spirit sees all that he has done.
And here it is, very well done.

And this is both union and separation: the sixth differentiation.

---

* Hyvrard omits 18. The numbers coincide with the verses of the Book of Genesis.

II

1 Negations, affirmation and their entire arsenal are perfected.

2 The spirit perfects, to the seventh differentiation, the work that he has done. He goes away from the seventh differentiation of all the work he has done.

3 The spirit praises the seventh differentiation, he consecrates it, for in it, he leaves the whole of his work that the spirit has conceived in order to act.

To a dead woman

They say I must bear another child. This time I will die of it. Without the blood that flows from my vulva, my head will dry up and I will be like the dead. They say I must bear another child. But I'm thirty thousand years old and I already have three daughters. The first was the mother of a mother of girls. She taught them obedience and resignation. She brought forth enough still born to fill up craters in the ocean. The first, the still born, was the mother of the dead. She had so many dead, she gave birth to her own mother. And her mother was older than the earth. Her mother was the mother of waters. The second was her own daughter. The third had none because she didn't want to remember. The third had none and she lost her name.

They say I must bear another child. They don't see that I'm already dead. What game are they playing, the man and the little girl? What game are they playing with their miserable cards? They're playing skip my turn. They play at letting me have my say. Since I can't play any longer, they let me say: Pass. They play at believing I'm still alive. They pretend not to see that in their game I'm the deadest card of all. The one that has a name and no place. The one that ends the game and begins it over again.

They say I must bear another child. But I can't bear any

more. I have met the Magician. He is the father of the child. Or another, or both of them. Or still a third, I'm not sure anymore. I confuse them. He is the boatman with his blue barque. He's the magician. He is the passage through motionless summer. The middle of the bed. The deep river. The red stones. Through his arms the path continues. His hands part the river. By his body the night is rent. He may be only the coachman of the woman in mauve. He's her companion. He holds the sulphur and the mercury. He tends his cauldron to dissolve time and space. He tends his cauldron to reverse the separation. He tends his cauldron to mix the suffering of the women and the tears of the stars.

They live near the lake. She has a veil and a parasol. He accompanies her without a word. I met them on the path. He was following her. She was laughing. She was singing. Jeanne will not have a child. Jeanne belongs to me. Jeanne will die. She lives in the marshlands. She feeds the birds. There she holds you prisoner. You come from another country. They have deported you. They've walled you up in the wine-press.

I'm coming to see you there, following the path. That's the end of the journey. The port of the wandering. That's where I'm coming to claim you. They have seated you in a wicker chair. They say you are paralysed and will soon die. They see only an old woman that they are forgetting. They're laughing at you. They call you the High Priestess. They see only an old woman whose death they are waiting for. They're hoping for it. They don't see your withered hands. They don't see the sign. They don't see your blue cloak. Nor the book you're holding in your hand. Nor the veil on the back of your head. They're hoping for your death. They believe that memory will die with you. That after you no one will remember her any longer. That after you're gone no one will remember our mother any longer. That after you there won't be anyone. They don't know we have escaped them. They don't know we love each other. They don't know you can't die because you are the guardian of death.

They play at letting me say: Pass. Here again is the bloody flow of words. The blood of the menstrual flow impossible to hold back. The summer I can no longer live. Compelling words tearing my mouth. Destroying my life. Dissolving my body. This is the season to write. The suffering is endless. Disaster is spreading quietly. Disaster to which I can't give consent. Disaster invading my life. Summers more and more violent. More and more empty. More and more transparent. Words pouring out of the body of this woman unknown to me. This woman with the severed fingers. This woman writing a story she doesn't know. The body inhabited by these hands that don't belong to me. The body inhabited by the river of words. These compelling words enriching my devastated lands. These compelling words that have taken my body to dwell in. These mechanical words. These words of plasma carrying globules to a heart unknown to me. To quicken what motionless body? To keep alive what already formulated thought? To reach the end of what reversal? Words up against the body of the machine moments before death. The lapping of words for the last speech. The lapping of words in the muddy water. The lapping of words before the eruption. Or no, rather, the lapping of wash in the wash-house. The work of the laundress of the night.

Words to say the body surrendered to summer. Here it is, summer again. The time of flowers by the thousands. So many insects I still know by name. The river bank and the stones children play games with. The sacrifice of the poplars holding the dampness of the countryside. The barges of the belly headed toward the floodgates of the arms. The path of the ladybirds meeting up with the first flies. The love of bicycles thrown down along the bank of the road. Flowery dresses. The laughter of cherries. Roses by the side of the well. Heart rending summer from which she has delivered me. Heart rending summer I can no longer live through. The nightmare of words. The death of love. Unreason.

Here again the regiment of words marching over the joy on my suspended hands. Deserters hidden in the thicket trying to survive. The regiment of words marching into what battle it has not commanded. Love of life sitting in the fields. The love of life watching them pass by. Here again the regiment of words shoulder to shoulder. They are going up toward the country I have come from. They won't recognise it. I meet them on the way down. I'm coming from the place they're going to. I pass them by with my severed fingers. They move off, up and over my madness. They can no longer reach me. I'm already dead. They sing aloud to give themselves courage. I don't hear them. Where are they going? If they knew they'd never go. Where are they off to, all these words between my severed fingers? All these words going up river toward the source. All these words going up toward the sea. All these words from the marshland of our memory. All these words bearing on their brow the mark of their own necessity. All these words turning back over the bridge of my hands. If they knew they wouldn't go. Why would I tell them?

They're heading up the bloody river of disaster, crossing through my mouth. They're going where they were before the separation. They're going off in search of the murderer. They say they know him. They say he lives in the Orient in the land of endless quest. They say he is called 'I Have Acquired' and he is still alive. Where are all these words going? If they knew they wouldn't go there. They're going to a land of motionless suns. To the time before time. To the place before the place. They're going to the chaos from before the creation of the world. Before writing. Before language. Before thought. They're going to the depths of memory. They're going to the country I come from. The country of eternity. The country of immobility. The country of confusion. The country of the order of things. To the time before the separation. The country of the dead.

Where are all these words going? If they knew, they wouldn't go. If they knew, how could they go? They're going back to the time of assembled opposites. To the time of a people so miserable they had nothing to live on but the fruits in the woods. To the time of a people so miserable, the memory is still with them. To the time of a people so miserable they still don't know how to separate.

A people with animal brains. Pain, not suffering. Pleasure, not love. Hunger, not misery. Fear, not anguish. A people trying to break out of chaos. A people breaking away from the night. From hunger. From terror. An attempt to dominate opposites. Stammering thought. An attempt. A beginning. An effort to separate themselves from the world. An effort to survive. Emergence.

Where are these words off to? They form a procession. They accompany a body going to burial. A body crossing the lake. A body in a blue barque. A body borne by the living. A body surrounded by insects. A body torn by the first separation. A body that nothing can satisfy any longer. A body of disaster. A body of love. A body of suffering. A body on the move. A body of hunger. A body of despair. A body from here. A body from elsewhere. A wounded body. A reunited body. A body demanding to be. A body of impossible being. A suffering that nothing can put a stop to any longer. Except the end of separation. Except death. Except love. Except the love of words like necklaces from tombs. Necklaces repaired. Necklaces looked at. Necklaces offered. To survive a bit longer. To bind up the wound. To bandage the tear. To take care of the scratches.

Where are all these words going? Since there will be no end? They have let me leave. But they say I will die anyway. They say I've already begun to die. They say there should be no crying out. They say what they had closed should not have been reopened. They say that's why they locked you up.

They're right. I'm going to die of these words. I'm going to die of being closed in. I don't want to. It's too late. There should be no consent. But I'm not the one. I'm not the one who cries out. I'm not the one who writes. It's another woman. She lives in my body. She doesn't have my horrid severed fingers. She loves the fields and the rivers. She loves the baskets and the cherries. She loves them so much that she wants to join them, be one with them. Her name is eternity. She's called memory. She's called death. She pursues me. She clings to me. She talks to me of former times. She talks to me of before. She settles down in me. She grows there. She invades my flesh. She takes my life.

Where are all these words off to? They're forming a procession. They form the black horses. They form the silver cords. They form the plumed harness. They form the hearse from the other side of the lake. The woman in mauve walks beside it. The woman in mauve walks under her parasol. The woman in mauve is singing: Jeanne will not have a child. Jeanne belongs to me. Jeanne will die. She is singing and laughing under her parasol. The mute coachman conducts the burial. The coachman accompanies her. He has a tail-coat and a hat. He's holding the reins in his hands. The woman in mauve is singing and laughing. She's walking in the grass in her beautiful slippers. She twirls her parasol. She says: Jeanne belongs to me. Jeanne will die.

No, there is no procession. There are no horses. There's no one. It's nothing. It's the wood knocking against the hearse. It's the coffin banging against my temples. There's no one. Nothing but the silent man who accompanies me in the disaster. It's nothing. I'm not really dead. This isn't a coffin. It's only a crematorium oven.

They have closed the door. My flesh sizzles. My eardrums are flayed. My eyes burn. It's nothing. It's my shut-in life. It goes on. And on. And on. And still goes on. I don't die. They don't open the door to take out the corpse. They don't open the door to take out the ashes. They don't open the door to scatter the suffering. This goes on for years. The woman in mauve is humming. The mute coachman accompanies her. This is the oven of the refractory earth. I hear the faint knocking of my coffin against the hearse.

It's nothing. It's not the coachman. Maybe it's the ferryman with his blue barque. The Magician with his big cauldron. This is the first transmutation. The first effort of thought to understand. The first effort of the body to transform matter. The first effort to reverse its resignation. It's nothing. It's the first death. That of lead. The heaviest. Withdrawal of the seal. The opening. The beginning of the sign. Resignation.

The first death to try and survive. For all the many years that I've been dead. So many years they have locked you up in the death-house. So many years they've been cutting our throats. So many years they have cut us off from the world. This is the first death to find the lost woman. The first death to get to the end of the path. The first death of lead melted in the cauldron.

What woman am I seeking at the end of the path as if the end was not before the beginning? What woman am I looking for? The one most dead? The one who has a name and no place? The one who has a place and no name? What woman is this in their game of cards?

Is it the Empress seated on her throne? Is it this woman with the red garment? Is it this woman with the blue cloak? This woman holding a sceptre in her hands? This crowned woman holding an eagle? This woman who tells me: find her again and you will understand. Find her and you will recognise her. Find her and you will seek her. Is that the woman lost for so many years? Is that the woman whose hands are all I can see of her?

No. That's not the colour of her dress. Nor of her cloak. That's not the colour of her garment. Then maybe she's the one running in the meadow. This woman of peonies and oats. This woman enamoured of a lizard. This woman dancing along the path.

You say she lives in the mountain country. The high marshes. The land of the lakes. You say she's blind from contemplating motionless suns. Deaf from hearing the moaning of the stones. Mute from giving birth to birds. Is that her village on its rocky spur? Is that her village between the black mountains? Is that her village so tiny that it can be held in the hollow of the hand? You have spoken to me of a communal wash-house in the middle of a square. But there are two of them. One to the Orient and the other to the Occident. There are two wash-houses. One in the direction of the mountain. The other toward the mountain as well. You have spoken to me of a wash-house. Is that where she does her washing? How could she with all that waterweed? You have spoken to me of a wash-house. Is that where she gets the water, the laundress of the night? Is she the woman I'm looking for? This woman who comes to the wash-house? Or is it the Empress? Or still another? Or are they one and the same? Perhaps there is only one. Perhaps she is the woman who runs in the meadow. Perhaps it is only Victorine doing her wash. Perhaps there is only this woman of thirty thousand years old. This woman who made them so afraid they locked her up.

I'm coming to see you in the death-house. We're waiting for your death. We're talking about your death. We're living your death. I have learned how long the years are for you. You remember only one of them. Thirty thousand years. You tell me that over and over again. You tell me that's how old you are. You have a red garment and a blue cloak. You have two keys in your hand and a book. You have two crowns on your head. One for matter. The other for man. Sometimes you ask what month it is. I've learned to count for you. I have also learned to subtract. You say you will live three or four more years. That that's enough. That after that I will have discovered. That I will recognise her. That I will recognise you. That I will recognise myself. That you will recognise yourself. That she will recognise herself. You say after that we will conjugate unity. We will come back to division. There will be no more mistakes in French. Language will recover its meaning. There where I goes. Where you go. Where she go. Where we went. No. There where we all have been. With no movement. With no action. With no tearing apart. There where we have been. Like an eternal state. Where one has been. Before being separated. You say I will recognise her. Whose hands are these in our reunited hands? Whose are they? Whose hair is this between our heads?

I'm coming to see you in the death-house in the castle by the lake shore. That's where they're keeping you locked up. At the edge of a marshland whose name you don't know. At the edge of a marsh where my pain ends. Maybe it does have a name. It's the dwelling of the unnameable. A garden with flowers. Poppies and peonies. Lilacs and jasmine. Iris too sometimes. And the irises of your eyes to calm my thirst.

I'm coming to see you in the death-house. The creaking of the gate for the one who pulls on it. The scrunching of the gravel for the one who walks on it. The door of the veranda for the one who opens it. The marquise on the top step. The ravens in their cage. Ravens by the thousands. The waiting. Time suspended. Your motionless body. The wicker chair. The chair as the only place. You no longer know time nor space. You are no longer anything but this stiffened body in the chair where they have confined you. You are no longer anything but this stiffened body under the plaid blanket. You're paralysed up to your chest. You can no longer move anything but your withered hands with their severed fingers. The fingers of the fig-tree you say laughingly. The fig-tree to cover up what bodies discovering their nudity? You're nothing any more but motionless waiting. The contemplation of your own death. And laughter. And tears. Your tears are as old as the earth. We're waiting for your death. This hair, whose is it? And these hands? And the rest of this mutilated body? They have separated us. But we love each other any way. Our hands make love. Our hair too. Perhaps our bodies as well. And your cavernous eyes. Your blue tinged eyes. Your eyes restoring my memory.

Why pretend to continue living? As if I didn't know I was going to die. As if I didn't know they have condemned me to protect what they can't tolerate. Death and rebirth. So many times. Every day. Every day so many times. The brain cradled between two waters. The drowned brain being reborn out of confusion. Every day the creation of the world. So many times that certain days I know nothing any more except the laughter of the ravens. Some mornings and evenings I know nothing but my open body giving birth to words. Until the pain is over. Until the end of living. Until the end of utterance. Since they have condemned me to say what they want to forget.

They have let me leave but they have severed my fingers. They have severed my fingers so I will no longer be anything but these severed fingers. So I will no longer be able to reunite or separate. So I will be nothing any more but evidence. So I will be nothing anymore but a memory. They have severed my fingers so I will keep between them all they have lost. Summer emptier by far than a quiet unmoving summer. The place of mutilation. The place of the fingers of this woman I don't know. Her severed fingers writing the world's memory. Her disembodied fingers have become their own body. Her headless fingers can't do anything anymore but touch and write. Her headless fingers that can't do anything anymore. They can only be. These fingers of eternity. These fingers they have severed from me that I might survive. These fingers crushed under the hammer of the first blacksmith. These fingers cut up in the machines. The fingers of the fig-tree you say looking at them. But you don't know anymore.

You don't know anymore what happened to this woman. You only know that at a given moment something did happen. A murder. Or a consent. You don't know anymore what happened. You know only that you have something to transmit. You no longer know what. An accident. An illness. A refusal. You're not sure anymore. The fingers of the fig-tree. You don't know anymore what that means. But it's by them that I recognised you.

These hands that can't do anything anymore except write. These battered hands. These hands of mortalitude. These hands of suffering. These hands of refusal. These hands of death. These hands which can no longer cook or rinse. Or embroider or dye. These hands whose face I never see. These hands which can no longer make anything but this music in the name of words. Just this music in the name of things. This music of the order of things. These hands which never stop.

These hands holding your hands. Whose are they? We don't know any more. Your severed fingers in my crossed palms. Your fingers of eternity in my hands of confusion. Your fingers of the fig-tree in my hands of despair. Your fingers of despair in my rings of fidelity. I have so many rings that they form a covenant. I have so many rings that, for me, they form an arch. For what crossing begun forever ago? For what crossing always beginning again? I have so many rings that one day they will bring us home. To the end of the path of our reunited hands. These disembodied hands. These hands without a mouth. These hands without eyes. Whose are these hands of the blind contemplating the light? These hands of the blind in the gaze of the drowned woman. These hands of words. These words of fingers severed from holding so long the rings of fidelity.

Whose are all these rings? They probably belong to the woman who is pursuing me. The woman who clings to me. The woman whose name is eternity. Memory. Death. She is probably also called Jeanne. But that's not my name. I call myself willow and cherry. Embankment and pathway. Field and meadow. She says her name is Jeanne. She clings to me. She takes my mouth to speak. She claims to know me. From the time before the separation. From the time before birth. She says that we were together in the belly of the world. That we ran together in the rivers. That we sang in the meadow. That we gathered blueberries. She says that was before they killed me. She says that we love each other. That we bear the same name. That we have the same body. She says I can't have forgotten.

Three hazel-nuts and a wistaria. That's all I have to offer her. She says she hasn't forgotten. They say that's not enough to survive. I also have a breach in my heart. They say that doesn't count. I had lots of raspberries but they crushed my hands with bridal crowns. I had lots of raspberries but they made me let go of them. Three hazel-nuts fallen over the neighbour's wall. I know that's not enough. I add a poplar. They say that still won't do.

They want words and suffering. They don't want cats on the dividing wall. Nor flowered paper in the bedroom. Nor glass tulips above the bed. They want suffering and blood. Torn flesh. A battered body. A bashed-in head.

She says I can't have forgotten her. She says we used to run together in the streams. But they have condemned me to run no more in the fields. They have condemned me to die of writing. They say three hazel-nuts and a wistaria blossom are not enough. I have nothing else to offer them.

Here again is the woman in mauve with her coma-causing needle. She has her lace dress and her parasol. She laughs when they tie me up along the wall. She says I will die since I have nothing else to offer them. Three hazel-nuts and a wistaria blossom. A cat on the dividing wall. A fallen leaf in the yard. It seems that's not enough.

I'm leaving for the country you don't know. The country I can't seem to get across. The country that separates me from the mountains of home. The country of clocks without hands. I know only the ones that plant needles in my flesh. I know only the ones that flourish in calcified bodies. Death spreading throughout my skull. I'm leaving for a country you don't know. The country of shifting sands where the dead weight of my despair sinks under. The country of my arms coming apart as the thread of my obstinacy unravels. The country of my flesh torn asunder as it becomes the walls of the house. Here again is the woman in mauve. She lives in the country of bodies without voices. The country of paralysed flesh. The country of walls, companions of our heads.

You call me but I can't hear. I speak a language you don't know. The body falling by the side of the bed. Eyes closed contemplating the night. I conjugate language that doesn't exist. The imaginary and its child the failurative. I speak stiff, the language she didn't teach me before she left. I speakstiff with all my stiffened body. I want to come back to you but I can't. Because of the red liqueur which is spreading in my blood. Because of the red liqueur which paralyses my brain. I can't come back to you. I'm slipping out to sea as I look back at the harbour. You're holding my hand but you're only holding on to wood. You're speaking to me but I hear only the walls. You're smiling but I'm on the other side of the mirror. The woman in mauve is carrying me off to her castle. And the silent coachman accompanies her.

This body which is mine. This body which is not mine.
The body which none the less is mine. This foreign body.
My only native land. My habitation. This body to conquer
again. This fatigue. This crushing. This daily grinding up.
This grinding up of the body in writing. This grinding
up of life which resists. This grinding up of the body
which can neither conquer nor capitulate.

This body which is gently falling apart. This body of
youth obstinately bent on death. This body of youth
entering into transparency. This cry of love that nothing
can satisfy. This devouring of self by self. The impossibility
of living. The croaking. The excess. The exaggerance. The
wounded life. The misery. I loved strawberries and cherries. Willows on the river bank. Poppies and butter cups.
Crayfish and water lilies. Swallows and oats. Bathing in
the streams. Fern clothing. Chestnut crowns. Hazel-nut
cabins. Laughter and song. Embankments and pathways.
I loved life and especially the raspberries. Raspberries.
Poppies. And above all the ladybirds. I loved life. What
happened? How did it happen?

What happened? What thorn picked up running bare
foot? What fall from a tree too high? What bite from a
venomous animal? What did happen? You probably know.
But you don't remember any more. Perhaps you don't want
to tell me. You say I'm the one who should know. You say
I'm the one who should recognise it. I loved life. I loved
the little girl who was three years old. I loved her body
in joy. What happened between the swallows and the
oats? What promise so distant that only the need for it
still remains? What happened? What little girl's commitment vowing not to be like them? What little girl's

commitment vowing not to give up. What little girl's commitment vowing not to grow up. Not ever. To remain forever the companion of streams. The lover of pebbles. The little sister of trees. What little girl's commitment vowing, but what on earth for, never to be separated? What has happened that keeps me from living? What has happened to this body so vast that nothing can satisfy it. Neither their lies. Nor their power. Nor their compromises. Nor their resignation.

This life that nothing can fill any more. Except its own need. Except the journey. Except the seeking for reunion. How does it happen that this other woman lives in me and is taking me away? How does it happen that in spite of me she still loves life? She's leading where I don't want to go. Crossing rivers. Still farther into the night. Toward words. Always farther into the night. Life wounded by its own life. The journey wounded by its own journey. The quest wounded by its own quest. The tearing apart of words that nothing can heal except straw hats and bales of hay. The wound. The confinement. The writing. The consent to slow death. The breaking of the seal. The opening. The resignation. The first death. The burning. The disaster. The hatred of this woman I don't know. The hatred of the woman who grows in me and hides the world from me with her flow of words. The lapping of writing. The journey across the fields of despair.

The journey of the oats pursuing the swallows. The journey of the stream pursuing the worn stones. The journey of the path pursuing the mountains. You hold your arms out to me. We're going to pick cherries. You have a basket, an apron and a ladder. You have a ladder against the garden wall. But my life has flown off in the wind with the birds. I'm already dead. I am the shard of love leaping the path. The barbed wire torn down to reopen the path. The slab torn off to give a name back to the unnameable. I am this body so vast that everything in it becomes word. This body so vast that everything in it becomes death. This body so vast that it is its own enclosure. So there may be no end to the despair. Nor to the wandering which leads me away from where I come from. Nor to the love of words. Nor to this brazier where everything burns except water.

The hatred of this body I can't manage to destroy. This body that flames without turning to ashes. This body always being reborn. This body of love. This body of memory. This body in fusion. This wounded body. This defeated body. This body held hostage. This body walking on wounded feet. This body opening to outstretched hands. This body that speaks a withered language.

They say I must bear another child. But if the red river no longer springs from my body how will they believe in the moaning of the stones? They say I must bear another child and I will not be separated from them. But it's too late. I have escaped them. It would be like suffering if it were not the misery of being. It would be like sadness if I didn't know the red death. It would be like despair if I didn't know acquiescence. The words of the abcess flowing from my wounded flesh. The words bleeding from a wound that nothing can heal. Since I'm not from here. Since white and red. Since washing and blood. Since I return endlessly to wash my pain in the wash-houses of bygone days. Since hunger and thirst, I can only go toward them. Farther and farther. More and more burned. More and more alone. Since flesh and joy. I'm going to the end of the path. It leads to the mountain across these words that flow from my hands without reaching me. These words that come not knowing how nor why.

Here again is this woman with her procession of words. This necessary woman whose hands are all I know of her. This woman with the severed fingers. This woman who murmurs in my eardrums: the fingers of the fig-tree. By this sign you will recognise me. Here again this woman I don't like. She threatens me with child-birth. She proposes death to me yet another time. Here again this woman I hate. This companion of my every waking moment. She's speaking through my mouth. She inhabits my body. She grows in me. She's the mother of my disaster. She comes forward with her hands outstretched to seize me. Her arms to stifle me. Her mouth to devour me. She's the mother of the forces of darkness. She's the mother of the three mad women. Destruction and her twin sisters, fusion and confusion. They go without dog or path. They have resignation as a companion. They say I can still be with them. They say I need only to give up. They say I have only to do as they do and I will not be separated. That was the first death. That of lead. The heaviest.

They say I must bear another child. That woman's body is the potter's wheel. That woman's body is the gardener's orchard. That woman's body is made to beget. They say I must bear another child, but this time I shall die of it. Without the red river, my land is only a desert. Without the red river my body is a rampart.

They say they're coming to get me. I haven't understood why. They want to take me to another house. It seems I went there before. I don't remember any more. It was by the lake shore. The house near the marshland. There were birds. Black horses. A coachman with a hat. There was also a woman in mauve. But there was a disaster. The lakes and the rivers disappeared. They branded me with a hot iron. They deported me. I never really understood why. I only know there was another woman with me. I don't know what became of her.

I think they walled her up in the wine-press. But she must have consented to it. They say it's not true. That she came from somewhere else. That she fled. That I didn't know her. But if I didn't know her, how does it happen that I remember? They say it's not true. That they have lost track of her. That they don't know what became of her. That she wasn't from around here. That she went back to her home. That they didn't know her. That she has been dead for a long time.

How does it happen that I remember? They say it can't be. That I can't remember. That they didn't lock her up. That she fled. That she went back to the country of lakes and mountains. That she returned to the country she came from. That she went back to the country of the birds.

If I didn't know her, how do I remember? Heredity. Genes. Chromosomes. They say they don't know what she died of. They say she had an illness. They don't know which one. They are forgetting acquiescence.

How does it happen that I remember a journey? Barbed wire in my flesh? Miradors in my skull? Cells in my body? How does it happen that I remember a journey? Algae from the fog in the womb of the night. One day they opened the doors and let me leave. You came looking for me. A light above a birthing table. A monstrous sun. A disaster. A buzzard. An eagle. A sparrow-hawk. A fine winter. They severed my fingers but they let me leave. You came looking for me to take me to the other side of the mirror. You came looking for me to take me with you.

No, I'm the one who comes looking for you. I'm the one who is coming to claim you. I'm coming to the death house to identify you. They didn't let me leave. I escaped one summer day. One day when the water was low enough to ford. I escaped into the heart of that motionless summer. I saw the path. I saw the path leading to the mountain. I understood why they were holding me back. I understood why she didn't want to let me be born.

I have escaped. Once and for all. When the river was red. I crossed it. In the middle of summer. The red waves dried up between the stones. On the shore of what sea? Pursued by what conquerors? I have crossed it to get back to you for as long as they have been separating us. And in the depths of this red transparent body I have seen reptiles of stone impregnating the dawn and showers of birds harvesting the clouds. I've seen the blind sharing light and the deaf transmitting sounds from another place. I've seen a procession of people groping along the walls of their prison. I've seen tongues torn out mumbling forgotten memories. I've seen nations raising up stones to implore the memory of the stars. I've seen tongues multiplying words until they have lost their meaning. I've seen tongues transmitting what they have lost. I have seen nations guarding knowledge and locking up those who guard it.

I have seen a nation of scholars seeking to know. I've seen a nation of scholars sever my fingers to preserve memory. I've seen a nation of scholars separate me in order to survive. I've seen a nation of scholars name me so as not to hear me.

I escaped across the red river from the heart of summer. I escaped to get back to you. You say that's not true. That I invented it. That it never existed. That it happened to someone else. To your mother or mine, how can one know. You say it happened to someone I didn't know. Then how is it that I remember? Perhaps it's because of that journey of thirty thousand years. You say it's not true. That we have always been here. And yet I can't find the broom or the dust-pan. Or the sheets or the towels. Or the dishes or the plates. I recognise only the frying pan and the stove. The paper. The wood. The coal. The order to light the fire. That's the only thing left to me of a former time. The first death. Resignation.

They say I must bear another child. If I don't bleed anymore, how will the stones live? If I don't bleed anymore, what river will irrigate the parched land? If I don't bleed, who will hear the sobbing of the abandoned gullies?

They say that I must bear another child. But this time I will die of it. I already have a daughter and she is grown now. And I think I took her to the death-house because she was crying in the night. You say that's not true. That she's still alive. That she lives with us. Then how does it happen that I remember a journey? Isn't she the one we went looking for? Isn't she the laundress of the night? Isn't she the woman in mauve in the meadow? Isn't she the one in the wicker chair?

You say that's not true and that my three daughters are grown now. Sometimes you even say they are old. Once you told me that one was already dead. But you couldn't say which one. I know it's not true. She's in the fields with her father. I have something to do now but I'm not sure what any more. Wash the floor? Sweep up the yard? I'm not sure any more. Look for someone? Yes, that's it. I must look for someone. A woman. Yes. A woman I left on the road. The woman with whom I used to run in the river. The woman with the chestnut crown. The woman they walled up in the wine-press. You say it's not true and that I didn't know her. Then how is it that I remember?

I have something to do, I don't know what anymore. Knit blankets for my three daughters? No. Just survive. Learn to survive the long journey. You say it's not true and that we have always been here. How is it that I can't get the stove lit? The paper. The wood. The coal. I can't do it.

This suffering goes on and on. Absolute misery. It would be enough just to give up in order to survive. But I can't. As if I had never been an adult. As if I had gone from childhood to old age all at once. As if I had gone from racing in the river to the roses of a mortal illness. The impossibility of compromising. The impossibility of lighting a fire. The refusal of the insane. Consenting to death. The impossibility of renouncing water. The impossibility of living.

How is it that they let me go? They didn't really. I escaped on the road with the cherry-trees. How come I remember that they walled her up? She must have consented. But if I consented why did I escape through the vineyards? Perhaps all this happened on the same day. The day the world was created. The day of the murder. Of the separation. Of the curse. Of the withered tree. All this happened the day they gave me a name. The day they broke the order of opposites. The day they fractured the order of things. The day they insisted on dominating the world.

You say that's not possible and that I know only the order of separation. How is it that I remember the day before the first day? You say I'm not the one who remembers it. That she's the one they walled up in the wine-press. How is it then that I remember the first day? The last day of the order of things. The last day of the order of opposites. The last day before the separation. How is it that I remember the day of the murder? When they were labouring in the fields. When they stripped the fallow lands and stoned the roads. When they eviscerated the mountain and razed the forest. How is it that I remember the first day when they melted the metals and sowed the seeds they had harvested? It's because I'm even older than the first day. It's because they haven't completely succeeded in locking me up. It's because she escaped while they were pursuing her up the path.

How is it that I remember? I have known so many dead, I have seen the mountains bringing forth ravens. So many dead, I have become like the stones the ravines call out to. So many dead, I have learned to cross over walls. So many dead, three or a thousand, I don't know any more. I only know how to count to seven to be able to return to the belly of the world. I have learned to count to seven in order to survive until the seventh day. I have known so many dead that I remember from before the first day. Because of this brain that opens and closes. This brain plunging into the river leaving the body suspended between two waters. The astonished body. The surviving body borne by the hands of the earth. The brain falling asleep so many times a day in search of its native land. The brain deserting cultivated lands to return to its home. The deaths of the brain. I have gone through so many. So many days. So many times. So many times so many days. How could I not consent to this remission?

They say this is an illness. It's only non-existence. The sleep of the brain. The dying brain. The brain reborn. The sea withdraws. The algae on the beach. Algae don't die. Algae preserve life. Algae don't die because they are the guardians of death. The forest of the night. The dream of water. The memory from before the separation. They say I have an illness. But it's only remission. Refusal of separation. Fusion. Confusion. Consent to death. But they have been confounding opposites and negation. From the second day of the creation of the world. Since they separated the water from the water. They have been confounding life and non-life. They call me by a name but I can't be named. I am from before the first day. From before the first name. From before the first naming. I'm what can't be separated. Wind and stars. Storms and thunder. The trembling earth and the blood of volcanoes.

They say I have an illness. The refusal of separation. The alternation of death and suffering. An endless death. A rebirth in order to die again one more time. An

alternation that never ends. So many times. So many days.
So many days so many times. So many times each day.
This sinking marks the hours. Two by two. To distress. To
death. To rebirth. An endless death. An agony. A wheel
whose hub is stationary. A wheel coming back endlessly to
its point of equilibrium. A wheel which is forever unmov-
able. A wash-house between two channels of running
water. The sleep of the spirit. Death to everything around.
Death passed through so many times that it has become
my own body. Death and suffering. How does it happen
that the ravens are flying above it all? How does it happen
that poppies still grow between the two? How does it
happen that suffering and death can still give birth to
daylight? How does it happen that there is enough night
to bring back the dawn? Each day. Each time. Each day
so many times. The alternation of suffering and murder.
Death and consent. Murder and death. Day and night.
Separation and fusion. The creation of the world and
chaos. How does it happen that I do not die? It's because
they confound opposite and negation. They confound
death and non-life. They confound water and sky. But
they're the ones who separated them. How does it happen
that I don't die? It's because I'm running through the
vineyards. I'm the body of the cherry-tree. The trunk of
the walnut-tree. The hand of the fig-tree. How does it
happen that I don't die? It's because I'm already dead.

Here again are the words. My enchanters. My companions. Words winnowing the night. The stones of the wine-
press. The blood of the hour-glass. Here again are the
words. Companions of everything. Except hope. Words I
can no longer silence. Words that bear on their brow the

mark of their own need. Words that have been pouring over the bridge of my hands. For all the centuries I have kept the memory of them. For all the centuries I have been holding on to them.

They say I must bear another child. They don't hear what the ravens are saying in the fields. They don't hear the ravens in the clefts of the rocks. They don't hear the ravens dropping walnuts. They talk about feminine writing. To exclude us. To keep the words for themselves alone. To keep discourse for themselves alone. To separate us again. As if the loved one and I had not the same words to say our love. As if he and I and the trees and stones. The earth and sea. The reptiles and birds. As if he and I, conversation of day and night. As if he and I were not both together reptile and bird. Separation and fusion. Earth and water. Of course not, they speak of feminine writing. Making quite sure to establish the difference. Making quite sure to separate us once more. Making quite sure to re-establish their order. To dominate by their order. By the power they have to separate. By the power they presumptuously claim to name things. They say writing and feminine writing. Logic and feminine logic. Intuition and feminine intuition. They speak of feminine writing. As if he and I did not speak the same language. As if we were not walking together along the road. As if we were not mowing the same grass. As if he and I were not picking up the same stones. As if the world were not our common dwelling-place. As if songs were not our mingled voices. Of course not. They must exclude to exist. They must enclose to believe themselves free. They must give names to believe themselves wise. They must separate to believe they are alive. They name in order to take over. They name in order to separate. They name in order to dominate. But they won't be able to do it. Because I'm going away down the path. I'm in their hands. In their game I'm the deadest card of all. The one that has a place and no name. In their hands I'm the card they can't name. The one that upsets their game. The one that doesn't play. The one that skips its turn. The one that only says: Pass.

In the clearing I have recognised the Emperor. He has a blue garment and a red cloak. He is seated on a golden cube. He has a helmet. A sceptre or a globe, I don't know. He has a white beard. He invites me to the castle among the courtiers. He owns the woods. But I walk up the path. He owns the countryside. But I run in the ravine.

They can't get to me anymore. The bridges they built have crumbled. The fences they put up have been knocked down. The horses they captured have run away. They think I will forget that I am the daughter of their servant because one day they interrupted their meal to turn toward me. Because one day they said to me: Come here my child. Don't be afraid. What's your name?

I'm the land of those with no land. The hand of those with no hands. The voice of those with no voice. They won't be able to buy me. They own the world. But they aren't rich enough. I'm too expensive for them. Grandmother's three fingers cut off in the machines. Grandfather going to work with hollow stomach. They won't be able to pay. It costs three pebbles and a blade of grass to balance my account. A pine-cone picked up on the path. A button torn off, one day of desire in pink clover. They won't be able to redeem me. I'm their memory.

They invite me to the castle. They want to teach me to dance the pavane. They offer me a mask for their costume balls. But we are millions. We have woven so many garments for them, they have no more to offer us. We have nothing but the buttercup's golden buttons on the cloak of the meadow. They want to teach me to dance the pavane, but we are millions. The doors of their castles are not wide enough. They want me to tell them a story but our own story is enough for us. They want characters. But we are the living and the dead. They want progression. But we walk in the night. They want characters, people, events, as they say a subject, a verb, an object. Because they must command. They must dominate. They must act. They insist on action. In order to measure. In order to contain. In order to separate. They absolutely insist on action. But I am a state of being. Writing is neither game nor commodity. Writing is to write what must be written. Writing is memory. Memoirs. Memories. Writing is memory. To increase knowledge.

They invite me to the castle. They ask who I am. I'm the public scribe. The invariable word which finally agrees. I am to writing what prostitutes are to love. The expression of collective disaster. The testimony to common misery. The dregs of society. I'm the dregs of literature. The bottom of the glass they can't empty. The residue of the decanting. What they can't swallow. The mother of buried sediment. The bitterness of our common memory.

They invite me to the castle. But I won't go. I'm going up the path. I have met the Hierophant. He has a blue garment and a red cloak. He has gloves. A triple crown. The first for matter. The second for separation. The third for fusion. I have met the Hierophant. He told me: You must have a name in order to be called. He said: In order to be called, you must be named. But I no longer have a name. I had one when I was living. They took it away from me. They said I didn't need it any more. They said the name of the man was enough. The Hierophant asks me my name. I don't have one any more. I did have one. Then two. Then none any more. Nothing but a wound. The unnameable. The Hierophant says one must be named in order to be called. I have neither a family name nor a first name any longer. Or rather I have a thousand. I am called death. Memory. Destruction. Consent. I am called fusion and confusion. Chaos and magma. They have taken my name. I have nothing but an opening in place of my heart. Nothing but a leaf in place of my hand. I have nothing but a trace in the middle of my forehead.

I have met the Hierophant. He says one must have a name in order to be called. He says in the game all cards have a name. Even the unnameable. But it must not be pronounced. Even the last one. The one before the first. The one that ends the game and begins it over again. All the cards have a name. Even the deadest. The one that skips its turn. The one that can't play. The one that just says: Pass. So I pick up a name. A lost name. A name nobody wants anymore. A lost name to tattoo on my arm. A lost name to embroider on my blouse. A lost name to inscribe over my door. He asks my name. I don't have one any longer. I picked one up. The one nobody wanted anymore. It transmits memory in the song of the ravens. It reflects the mountain in the hissing of the serpents. It crosses over the wall of the wine-press. Because of the separated one and the excluded one her mother. I have picked up a lost one. It's yours. It's mine. Nobody wants it any more. It belongs to me.

All cards have a name. Even the deadest one in their hands. All the cards have a name. Even the Lover on the path. Even the Lover. His name is François. The Lover is François at the crossroads. François between these two women, you and me. François and his many-coloured garment. François under the arrow of love. François under the arrow of the sun. François between two women who hold out their arms to him. He chooses a third one. Neither you nor me. He chooses a third. One he doesn't know yet. She's not completely born. She reunites them. He chooses the mother of them all. The laundress of the night.

The mountains. The vales. Sometimes the valleys. The river and its tears of gravel. Willows. Acacias. Hazel-nut trees. The stream and its trail of crayfish. Corn. Tobacco. Alfalfa. This is another country. The fountains and their splashes of frogs. Meadows. Walnut-trees. Fields. Apple-trees. Ponds and their puddles of water lilies. The vineyard and the pear-trees. The wash-house and its trail of wash.

The mountains. The vales. The valleys. François looks at the village of his beloved. The vale of his beloved. The roads of his beloved. Sun and oats. Wheat and ripe fruit. The path and the forest. Sun and the wash hanging out to dry. The house of his beloved. So small at the end of the village. So small at the edge of the fields. So small beside the wash-house.

François looks at his beloved. But he doesn't have a house to offer her. He has no bed to offer her. He has no fields to offer her. François the Lover and his multi-coloured garment. The landless peasant. The farm-hand. The servant. François the poor. Too poor to offer a place to his beloved.

François the poor and Victorine the simple. Victorine the grass. Victorine the stone. Victorine in the house of her father. Victorine doing her father's wash. Victorine the bed, the kitchen, the wash-house. Victorine along the road. François looks at his beloved but he has no house to offer her. The love of a farm-hand and a simple girl. The love of grass and insects. Roads and stones. Steps and songs. Oaks and birches. The love of two trees mouth to mouth. François the poor marries Victorine the simple.

A day of festivity. Victorine's straw hat. Her mauve dress. François' blue trousers. The meadow. The grass run rampant. Lying fallow for a moment. Victorine's hand on François' arm. Victorine's hand and François' smile. Victorine's mouth and François' laughter. The oats. The clover. The alfalfa. The bread in the wicker basket. The wine on the checked tablecloth. The bread and wine in their sharing hands. Victorine's laughter and François' embrace. François' hand on Victorine's ankle. The mountain. The meadow. The flowers. Animals wandering about.

The Lover in the multi-coloured suit. The Lover at the crossroads. The crackling of the oats. The poppies. The mauve dress. The blue trousers. The scratches of pebbles on flesh. The torn dress, the blood on the dress. The poppy in the oats. The trees and the rivers. The ladybirds and the crickets. The hat and the scarf. The cosmation.

She's going to bear a child. They're going to have my three daughters. The first one to die. The second to be dead. The third to forget. They're going to have my three daughters. But he has no roof to shelter them. Apple-trees. Pear-trees. Hazel-nut trees. He has no bed for them to lie in. The rivers. The fountains. The wash-houses. He has no land to nourish them. Tobacco. Vineyards. Mushrooms. He has married his beloved. But she stays in her father's house. François the farm-hand has married his beloved. But he doesn't have a house. He returns to his masters.

Victorine the simple gives birth to my first daughter. She gives birth to my first daughter in her father's house. She gives birth to the first girl. The dead one. Her father's house is so small it has only two rooms. It's so small it's just big enough for the child. So small it can be held in the hollow of the hand.

François the servant. François the poor. François the farm-hand. François comes to see her. François comes to see his wife and his daughter. But he can't stay with them. François has no house. François has no land. François returns to his masters. Victorine stays with her father. Victorine is in pain.

I'm in pain. The house is deserted. The woman in mauve is on the balcony. Vines grow over the façade. The vines haven't dried up yet. François is not here. He's in the field. He's in the field far from here. He's in the field on the other side of the vales. The house is empty. It's the place where birds come. The womb of the winds. It's where I live. The woman in mauve is on the balcony. I hear her laughing. She sings: Jeanne will never go back in the house. Jeanne belongs to me. Jeanne will die. The silent coachman is beside her. He is stirring his cauldron. He's watching over the sulphur and the mercury. He's watching over the firing. It's nothing. It's the second transmutation.

It's nothing. It's only the second death. A rending of living stone. A suffering so tragic that its abeyance alone would cause astonishment. It's nothing. Youth locked up. The body walled in. Life disfigured. The second death. That of pewter. Submission. The second death. Bodies bent over sinks. Bodies crouched over kitchen floors. Bodies always washing the same dishes. It's the second death. That of pewter. That of broken bodies. Of bodies locked up. Of bodies killed. François isn't here. I'm in pain.

Submission. An old wound. A wound cauterised with the hot iron of the lie. It won't ooze. It won't be anything but a presentable scar. It keeps me from walking. The lie keeps me from walking. It's nothing. There's no place to walk. I must simply stay here and smile. I must smile because a sad woman is a sad thing. There's nothing anymore but the woman in mauve on the balcony of my pain. There's nothing anymore but the woman in mauve laughing and singing: Jeanne belongs to me. Jeanne will die. After her no one will remember Victorine and François.

Deaths. I know so many of them. The first of lead: resignation. The second of pewter: submission. It's nothing. They've killed the love of life. But they haven't been able to dry up the rivers. And I have become like them. They haven't been able to put out the light of the stars and they illuminate the night. They have only severed my fingers and they restore my life.

They have severed your fingers. You no longer know why. You think it's an accident. One day the machine turned over. One day the press pulverised your hands. A day of deportation. One day when they had already torn you from your place in a former land. You no longer remember. The metal-press or the wine-press. The machine or the machination. You think it happened before the deluge. The day of the murder. The day of the curse. The day of the drying out. The days they separated you to be able to live. You don't remember when anymore. You see only your ruined hands. Laughing, you look at them and say: the fingers of the fig-tree. You don't know what that means. That's why you repeat it.

I'm in pain. Such pain. They have made a lie of love. A possession. Something that goes without saying. Something owed. They have made love a word to disarm us. A mask for power. A cover for injustice. They have forgotten its needs. The waiting. The burning. I'm in pain. Such pain. Such pain from the pangs of love. Such pain from this suffering devastating my impoverished lands. Ravaging my cultivated garden. Endlessly breaking up the body of the world. My head splitting against rocks of speech. My head splitting against the wall of my cell. My head splitting in their dishes full of commonplaces.

One has only to stop loving to become non-living like them. One has only to stop loving to end this suffering. They don't hear the howling in my head crushed under the stones of their conformity. I'm the faulty piece. Outside of time. In the body of words. In the blood of objects. In the moaning of the trees the days of the stripping. In the lament of things on days of evil doing. In the revolt of the senses on days when all appearances are fraudulent.

I'm the faulty piece. The one you were making when

the machine turned over. You had it in your hand when they locked you up. It is unlocking words which aren't ashamed of themselves. This faulty piece resisted the belly. At the creation of the world. At birth. It hung on in the time of chaos. In the time of the order of things. In the time of the organisation. It resisted the parting of the waters. It can't forget the suffering of the drying out.

You caress my brow with your withered hands. I caress your white hair with my severed fingers. The wave passes and diminishes. Once more the red death is diluted. My hair dries out of the water. A hand steers the barque. Yours probably. Or that of François. Or both. The woman in mauve is finally silent. Rebirth. Morning returns. Mornings always return in spite of suffering. Mornings return at night's end. Mornings have only to be. To continue to live. To walk again a little. To go and die a bit farther off.

Life's suffering which is implacable. Life's suffering which never capitulates. The suffering of the living. Suffering which bonds the murderer and the victim. Suffering, the bond of murder. The blood of murder. The monk of murder. The suffering of not being able to give up. Whatever for? Because of a mark on the brow. Because of the mark of a stone. Suffering crushing my life in its search to know what happened. Searching for the woman locked up in the wine-press. Searching for the day of the murder. Searching for the cause of the murder.

What did happen? Where has this woman gone who used to run with me over the stones? In what forest have I lost her? At what turning in the path did they catch her? Why didn't I defend her? Why did I hide in the bushes?

Why did I let them do it? Where is this three-year-old woman who loved life?

They say I must bear another child. They don't see my misfortune. They don't see the red death in the meanderings of my brain. The red spots on my nightshirt. The clothes rinsed out in the wash-house. What does bloodied mean? It means soiled with blood. She turns away from it. Bloodied. Soiled. Bloodied she turns away from it. She doesn't like my body. She doesn't like my blood. She doesn't like me. It's the beginning of the night. No. It has been night for a long time. Since the murder. Since the crossroad. Since they caught her. Since they locked her up in the wine-press. The red death in my brain. The bloodied clothes in the wash-house. I can't live. The pain. The distress. Of every day. No, not quite. Sometimes a small moment of happiness. Because of the trees. I know one in the garden. I know one but I don't know its name. I know one in the middle of the garden. It protects the house. It's the tree of the assassin. It has fingers stretching up toward the sky. You say it mustn't be cut down for without it life would no longer be possible. You say it mustn't be cut down for the whole village would dry up.

They say the tree hasn't given shade since the day they severed your fingers. They say that was the day she escaped. They're no longer sure when that was. They no longer know if they locked her up on the road to the vineyards or if they killed her on the path. They say it's not important for in any case she's dead. They say they no longer know if they locked her up or if she escaped while throwing stones at them. They say it's not important since

in any case she can't be cured. She loves only one language.
The one they didn't teach her. The one that has the body
of poppies and cornflowers. The one with the crowns
braided so tight you can hear them weeping on the day of
the harvest festival. She can't be cured because she loves
only one language. The language of trees and birds. The
one they locked up. The one that sifts the true from the
false. She speaks only one language. The one she knew
before going with them. The hand of speech to embrace
the body. The arms of words wide open. The mouth of
verbs to call out the light. They say she knows only one
language. A language so impoverished that it still har-
bours lizards and crows. Insects and serpents. Flowers and
pebbles. They say she knows a language that can say earth
and water at the same time.

They say that's not true. That I will never amount to
anything. That I'm not learning grammar. The only thing
I know about French is the metallic clink of the ruler
against the table. The odour of wood. Ink spots. Steel
pens. She looks sternly at me. She doesn't like me. She
doesn't like anything. She doesn't like the words she
pronounces. She tortures sentences. She attaches words
any which way. She wants me to do the same. I'm bored.
The metallic clink of the ruler on the table. A subject, a
verb, an object. Why a subject? I'm ravine and mountain.
Spring and river. Fields and insects. Wind and torrent. A
subject for what? Why does she want to separate me from
the world. I'm bored. Her stern look. The falling asleep. A
subject. A verb. What for? What do they want to move?
What do they want to overturn? What do they want to
modify? I'm bored. A verb. What for? There is only one

verb. It means to live and to die. It exists only in the infinitive. A subject. A verb. An object. What for? How pretentious. A subject. A verb. An object. I'm bored. I pretend to answer them. I'm dreaming. Dreaming about the time before. About flowers. About stones. About roads. She looks stern behind her glasses. She doesn't like me. She doesn't like anything. She positively insists on making the plural agree. She's wrong. It's all together that we make the one. She wants me to make the participle agree. It can't be done. It's invariable. I'm bored. I'm bored to death. I'm absolutely dying. I'm dying from the red death. She's slicing up my sentences. Blood spurts out. She decapitates my words. They weep. She underlines my mistakes. She puts red everywhere. My life is bleeding in the margin. My life is bleeding in the last lines. My life is bleeding in the annotations. They want me to become like them. But I can't make invariables agree. Nor conjugate eternity. Her stern look. Her contempt. Her shouting. Jeanne Hyvrard will never amount to anything. Zero in grammar. Zero in French. Zero in reading. I don't care. I hear the words I have hidden in my desk crying. The metallic clink of the ruler on the table. Her glasses. Her stern look. Her hair pulled back tight. I'm bored. I live in words they don't know. She knows the rules. But she doesn't know the red death. I'm bored. I'm disappearing. I'm fleeing to the depths of myself. All the way down. I'm not learning anything. I'm pretending. In the depths of my body, I'm escaping them. I'm leaving them the iron collar they put me in. I'm fleeing. They have nothing in their records but my dead body. I'm going far far away. I recite their laws but I live in a country they will never visit. The country of

motionless suns where bodies unite in ways that don't exist.
I'm not learning anything. I'm escaping them. I'm surviving. It's my death they are recording in their report. My
death they pass from class to class. My death they honour
on prizegiving day.

The only thing I'm learning is the third death of the
brain. That of iron. That of strength. Skins wounded by
things harder than themselves. Flesh torn by those better
armed than itself. Bodies broken by those stronger than
themselves. I'm learning nothing. The third death. That of
iron: oppression. Defeat, not capitulation. Not surrender.
Not adherence. Defeat. The third death of the brain under
oppression. They break my teeth in the imperative. They
dry out my hands in the conditional. They sever my fingers
in the subjunctive. I sing in the indicative. I sing on the
red tile floor of the kitchen. What woman is this in mauve
standing near her stove? What woman is this cooking my
head in her cauldron? I sing in the indicative but they
don't want me to live in my body. I singstiff. I want to
laugh and dance but she tells me to keep quiet. She tells
me not to budge. I'm too little to. I'm too big to. I'm never
the right age. I no longer live anywhere. I'm always on
the move. I conjugate in the mode of my distress. The
failurative. The past imaginary. The pluperfect pain. I'm
walking toward you. You singtoward holding out your
arms to me. I'm walking toward the wash-house. She
singdeaths rinsing out her wash. I'm walking toward
you. I'm walking toward her. We get farther and farther
away from each other. I'm escaping them completely. I'm
fleeing. I'm escaping them. They violate my mouth making it a portal to the death-house. That's where they teach

me their withered language. I watch her going by in her wheel-chair. I push her as I walk. I recite whatever she wants me to. I sing. You sing. She sings. It's no longer worth the trouble. I'm not singing any more. I have disappeared into the two-way mirror through which she's watching me.

Death. Death on a grand scale. Death in tears. The last crossing always begun again. The world torn apart. Reason shot through the heart. The river dried up. Ravens walking over my dead eyes. Swallows nesting in my empty head. Wind blowing through faulty grammar. Face disfigured by howling. Arms charred by torment. Body possessed by suffering. The trees' hands stirring. The trees shake their little bells. The trees say she can't die. She's already dead. A tragedy. A drama. A misfortune. No. A daily event. The body of François struggling desperately to give me back life. The hand of François trying to parcel out the day. The silence of François giving meaning back to words.

Death crossed over so many times that I know it by name. I watch her mauve dress and her parasol passing by. She has made me like herself. They have given me her name. I can now no longer live or die. I'm nothing any longer but this suspension. The body drowning between two waters. Waterweed surrounds my gestating body. The rivers companions of my night. So many times that I have to consent. So many times that I no longer have an alternative path. So many times that I will finally die of it. So many times that if I don't consent I will die.

So many times the body of the night. The body of death. The body of memory. The body of despair. The body of tragedy. The body of survival. The absence of an ending. The body rotting on its own heap of corpses. The body of the crematorium for its own brazier. The body of perdition by its own exigency. The body that can't capitulate or die anymore. The body that can't conquer or surrender. The body suspended. The body of murder containing its own liberation. The body of illness containing its own health. The body of suffering containing its own relief.

Suffering that only stops when your head is in your hands. When the word is redressed. The gesture rectified. Sense made of things again. Of every word. Of every sign. Of every fact. This suffering which only ends when broken things are fixed. The muted word repeated. The unexpected gesture made again. When arms that have been closed open again. Separated flesh united once more.

Waiting that goes on and on. Waiting each day. Waiting each day so many times. Waiting starting over again. Waiting a lifetime. Waiting suspended between death and rebirth. But François has no house to shelter his wife and a girl child. He has no house. He has no fields. He has no bed. François has no house but he has a wife and child. He already has the first daughter. He has a little girl who plays with her mother the simple one. François the poor. François the farm-hand. François the peasant without land.

François the poor and Victorine the simple. Victorine who has passed through all the deaths. The first of lead: resignation. The second of pewter: submission. The third of iron: oppression. François the farm-hand and Victorine who has passed through all the deaths.

The love of the poor and the simple. He's coming for

her to take her with him. To take her to share his triumph. So she will get in the Chariot with him. So she will come out of herself. So that together they might go along the path. The Chariot with its two big horses. They have no reins since they know where to go. One for the day and the other for the night. One for land. The other for water. One for separation. The other for fusion. He has two big horses to pull the Chariot. He has two big horses for the two sides of the world. They're looking in the same direction. François the poor and Victorine the simple. He's coming for her in the Chariot. He's taking her with him. Out of the land of slavery. Through the red river. Through the ford of motionless summer. Through the breaking of the waters.

If I were Victorine they would have let me go. But they let me go because of the ten wounds in my body. They did let me go. The Chariot is taking me through the red river. Through the waters. Through death.

The love of Victorine and François. He found a house. He found a piece of land. He found a bed. He's taking her in the Chariot toward another valley. He has fields to cultivate for a master. He's taking his wife and daughter. His wife the simple one and his daughter the dead one. François the peasant without land. François the tenant farmer. He's taking his wife and daughter to another valley. On the other side of the mountain. On the other side of the rocky spur. On the other side of the black spur. On the other side of the stony spur. François the tenant farmer and Victorine the simple. And their daughter the dead one.

Victorine works with François. Victorine helps him

farm the land. When she can. In so far as she can. She is
ill. She's often ill. She thinks about the village she has
left. About her father's house. About the wash-house.
About the frogs. The ditches. The roads. The grasshoppers.
About the wash in the meadow. The crickets. The raspberries. She often remembers the mountain. The forest.
Mushrooms. Squirrels. Hedgehogs. Foxes. She remembers
the time before. She doesn't forget. How could she forget?
She's ill.

They say she's ill. That her health is fragile. That she
shouldn't really have worked. She's ill. Not every day. The
days of the frogs, the water lilies and the reeds. She's ill
from the water in the high valley. From the marshland
beyond the village. From the wash-houses. She's ill from
the language. She doesn't know how to speak French.

She's courageous. She works anyway. She works with
François the tenant farmer. She is tall and beautiful. She
is also pregnant. She's going to bear another child. She's
going to give birth to Jeanne again to be my second
daughter. She has a first daughter the dead one. She is
going to have a second daughter to be dead.

It's September. Haymaking again. September in the
faded meadow. September in the grass piled up in the
Chariot. September in the two big horses. September in
the jolting of the wheels. September in François' Chariot.
September in Victorine's dress. September in the distended
flesh. September in the picked flowers. September in the
pitchforks and rakes. Victorine is in pain. She's lying on
top of the hay. She's lying in the Chariot. The meadows.
The sun. Haymaking again. Crickets. Ladybirds. Bees.
Beehives not far off. Butterflies. Beetles. Victorine on the

Chariot. Victorine in pain. Victorine calls out. Victorine moaning. Mute François drives her. François drives the horses on the way to the farm. The horses of separation and fusion. The horses of day and night. The horses of earth and water. They have no reins. They know where they're going. Victorine is in pain. It's September in her belly. Her hands on her moaning flesh. Her hands on her dress. Her hands in the hands of François. There are no reins in the Chariot. The horses are going toward the wash-house. Victorine is moaning. François says nothing. François drives without reins. François returns to the farm. It's the season of haymaking again. The faded fields. They arrive. They have crossed the road. They have crossed the red river. She's in pain. He takes her in his arms. Her belly is distended. Her painful belly. Her belly in labour. He takes her belly. He carries her into the house. He enters the house. He gets her settled in the house. It's the end of the afternoon. She has been making hay all day. She is about to give birth. It's September. The flies. The ants. The spiders. September in the farm-worker's house. The time of figs and grapes. The time of fusion and separation. Victorine is going to give birth to her daughter. And François says nothing. François never says anything. François stirs the wooden spoon in the cauldron of summer.

They say I must bear another child. But this time I will die of it. I already have a daughter. They say I must bear another child so there will be at least one who will remember. They say the first one is supposed to die. And there must be another to be dead. They say if there are no more dead, they will not be able to live. They say that in each generation one must be separated. To bear witness to the murder. To guard death. To keep them safe. They say that in each generation there must be one to wither away. So there will be no more separation. To be the tree of the murderer.

They say that one is necessary for the sake of Justice. She has a red dress and a blue cloak. She has a sword and a scale. A necklace and a crown. They say there must be a dead one for the sake of Justice. They say there must be two daughters. One for the sword and the other for the scale. One to die and the other to be dead. One to live and the other to be a witness.

They say you must be born for there must be one to be witness to the disorder. There must be someone to be locked up. There must be one who will take death upon herself.

And Victorine delivers another consenting female for the sake of Justice for she says: There must be two daughters. One to die. The other to be dead.

They say that is the reason you must be born. Because of the second half of the reason. They say you must be born to be the opposite. Not the negation. You must be born to be dead. To be the third term between power and identity. Between separation and fusion. Between earth and water. You must be born to be your own opposite. The splitting open. The joining together. The door.

Victorine engenders her second daughter. It is September. The time of figs and grapes. September in the farmyard. September in the kitchen. September in the bedroom. Victorine doesn't forget the beetles and the periwinkle. She is ill. She goes to bed. She stays in bed. Weeks. Months.

They don't understand what's wrong with her. They say she's ill. François is courageous. François finds a bigger farm. François takes his wife and his two daughters. The first to die. The second to be dead. He's going to have a third. Victorine is going to give birth to my third daughter. To forget. But she doesn't forget. Not the frogs. Nor the fountains. Nor the wash-house. Nor the wash. She doesn't forget. They say she is ill. She is ill from love.

Victorine stays in bed. She stays there doing nothing. They don't know what's wrong with her. Her memory is ill. She doesn't know how to separate. She can't forget. She can only transmit. Nobody knows what Victorine is suffering from. Perhaps it's just from her three daughters. The first to die. The second to be dead. The third to forget. She is ill. From the wash and the wash-house. From the kitchen and the cauldron. From the frogs and the raspberries. From her father's house and the ravens. From the woman in mauve on the balcony. Or from dreams. Or reeds. Or marshlands. From language and from silence.

Perhaps from poverty. From François' work. From the work which is not enough to raise three daughters. Victorine is ill. They don't know what's wrong with her. She falls sometimes. She falls in the fields. She falls in the yard. She falls on the road. She isn't able to work. She stays in bed. Weeks. Months. Years. Nobody knows what's wrong with her. She's ill from servitude. From unravelled skeins. Skeins wound on the arms of the little girls. Skeins dragging along the little girls. To teach them not to dance anymore. Not to run anymore. Not to move anymore. To teach them only to transmit memory. Renunciation.

Acquiescence. They are right. It's a hereditary illness. What
is it? Slavage. Slavance. Slavery. Slavement. Slavation. An
illness inherited along with the skeins of wool held
together by the arms of little girls. Mothers, mothers, let
me run in the roads and fields. Mothers let me go into the
river. Mothers let me go out. Where do you want to go,
little girl? Where do you want to go? Woman's place is near
the fireplace. Woman's place is on the balcony. Woman's
place is in the kitchen. Where do you want to go, little
girl? Your place is with us behind the table of our masters.
Mothers, let me go. Put your skeins over the backs of the
chairs. Don't keep my little girls' arms motionless any
longer. Let me run up the path.

Victorine is ill from love. She wants to run in the river.
The little girl is ill but she doesn't know yet that she's condemned. The little girl holds the skein of wool. François
goes off in the morning his stomach hollow. François
comes home starving in the evening. I haven't done anything. I've just stayed in bed. The little girl is ill. But she
can't die. She mustn't run up the path because after me
she's the one who must guard death. François stirs up the
ashes in the stove but it's no use. There's no more coal.
The little girl is cold. I'm cold too. My head is getting
more and more empty. I don't remember anymore what it
is that I must look for.

The little girl is six. They send her to her aunt in another
valley. They send her to the other side of the mountain. To
guard the pigs. She's six years old in the fields. Six years
with the pigs. They guard her or she guards them. How
can one tell? She goes along with them up the road. Up
the slopes. Into the ditches. She goes bare foot with them.

One day she falls asleep. Apple-trees. Grasses. Buttercups. They tear up her hat. They eat it. Butterflies. Tobacco. Her aunt doesn't want to buy her a new one. Her aunt is too poor to buy one. Wheat. Oats. Rye. Sun. She has a headache. She can't buy her one. She shouldn't have fallen asleep. She's six years old. The pigs have eaten her hat. She's crying in the meadow. She's ill. She's rubbing her forehead between her hands. Her hands aren't withered yet. Her fingers aren't severed yet. She doesn't know yet that she's the one they have condemned. She's the one who must hold on to the memory. She doesn't know yet that she's dead. She has a headache. She no longer has a hat. She sits in the shade of the fig-tree. To protect herself.

She guards the pigs. Victorine guards death. François guards the land. The first daughter keeps house. Victorine is ill. She's paralysed. The doctors say she has an illness. They don't know what it is. Memory? Consent? Love? She stays in bed. Sometimes she gets up. They don't understand why. Because of the frogs. The raspberries. The periwinkles. François' hands. The apple blossoms at the window. The butterflies. No. Because of the lizard. She gets up. She begins to work. They don't understand why. They say she has an illness. They don't know what it is. She hurts in the trees and the serpents. In the stones and the roads. In the fountains and the birds. She hurts in the blueberries of the forest. In the pine-cones. In the mushrooms. She hurts from life. The lizard comes to see her. He speaks to her. He speaks to her of the other place. He speaks to her of the past. He speaks to her of the separated country.

The little girl talks to the pigs and Victorine to the

lizard. François cultivates the land. He goes off in the morning his stomach hollow. François the tenant farmer raises his three daughters. He hasn't eaten enough. He's hungry. He leaves in the morning. He returns in the evening. Victorine stays in bed. The little girl watches over the pigs. She's not learning anything. She doesn't forget anything either. She stays as untamed as they are. François wants to take her back home. François wants to put her in school.

She returns home. She doesn't know how to speak French. They want to teach her to speak French. They lock her up in a school. She's bored. She bangs the ruler on the table. She stands on the benches. She breaks pens. She tips the ink-pot over. She talks to the birds. The trees stretch out their arms to her. The fig-tree sings her a mournful song. The river tells her the story of a man in the belly of a fish. The story of a man under a tree. The story of a man under a dried-up tree. She can't keep still. She won't stay seated. She won't stay quiet. She speaks the language of horses and oats. Of insects and flowers. Of sheep and poppies. They want to make her speak French. She won't. She doesn't know how. She can't.

She escapes, laughing, into the vineyard. They pursue her. They want to teach her French. Grammar. Chemistry. Arithmetic. History. Geography. Time and space. She runs away through the vineyard. They want to catch her. They want to teach her the order of separation. She doesn't know. She can't. She won't. Because of what tragedy in the brain? Because of what lack of conformity? She's running among the vines. Toward the almond-tree. Toward the walnut-tree. Toward the fig-tree. Toward the stones. Toward the mountain. They are on her trail. But they won't catch her.

They won't be able to catch her. It's too late. She has escaped them. We have escaped them. We women have recognised each other. We wear the same sign. We don't know how to speak French. Is she the ten-year-old woman who used to run up the path with me? Is she the one whose hands are all I know of her anymore?

What are they playing? What are they playing with their miserable cards? What are they playing? They're playing skip my turn. They're playing at letting me say: Pass. They're playing at pretending to believe that I'm still alive. Not so. I'm running up the path. I'm running to meet the Hermit. I'm running to meet that old man. He has a red garment with a blue cloak. He has a walking stick. A lantern to light my night. He says: One must travel the road alone.

What sinking boat is this with nothing left but the rudder? What is this vessel of suffering with only its helm above water? What is this barque that has just enough water to keep from sinking? Just enough water for my two hands holding the wheel. My frozen hands. My red hands. My hands in the storm. The course lies straight ahead. What card was that thrown upon the deck of my boat one bloody day? One stormy day? A day of distended belly. A day of being so ill that I know nothing but this wheel between my clenched hands.

The storm is for me alone. They won't be able to go with me. They don't know how to read the map because they don't see the course. They can't hold the wheel because they don't close their hands tight enough. They can't cross the deck because they don't know the water.

The storm is for me alone because the wheel never veers off course. Because it crosses over my body to become the meadow once again. Because, crossing over my body, it becomes the sky once again. Because, crossing over me, it makes me broader still. The storm is for me alone. I am the bridge.

One must make the voyage alone. The unique voyage. The great voyage. Death puts a sign on those who belong to her. Death puts a sign on those she wishes to protect. So that people will recognise them. So that nobody will kill them. A sign on the brow. A sign of blood. The mark of a stone. The mark of the living. The rampart on the brow. The Hermit tells me: Don't wait. Don't wait for them. You must go alone.

So I run off into the vineyard, alone. They're behind me. They are pursuing me. They say I mustn't run away. They say I'm not really sure what. That I must bear another child. But I can't. I must find the woman left on the road. The three-year-old woman. The ten-year-old woman. The woman who is I'm not sure how old. The woman who was running with me up the paths. The woman from the shacks. The woman with reeds. The woman with baskets. The woman who was with me. Such a long time ago. The woman who was always there. What has become of her? Do you know? Perhaps it's written in your book. Perhaps she's the one hidden behind your veil.

Perhaps she's the one running in the vineyard. They say they're going to lock her up, since she can't live with them. She's consenting to it. She can neither live nor die. She consents to death because there's no other way out. They are destroying her shacks. They're tearing up her clothes made of fern leaves. They're taking apart her chestnut crowns. She consents to being locked up.

What happened? How old is she? How old is this three-year-old woman? Thirty thousand probably. No more. As old as speech. No older. She consents to being locked up. She doesn't want to speak French because of her mountain body. Her river eyes. Her head of stars. She consents to being locked up for the sake of memory. To protect it.

They're pursuing her up the path. They say she escaped. That she escaped them. That she ran away. They say she must die. That she's not from around here. That she comes from another country. That she comes from the sea. They say she must die since she is the daughter of death.

Victorine stays in bed. She has an illness. They don't understand. The apple-trees. The fields. The wash-house. She has an illness. The illness of love. She can't forget. She's running up the path but she's holding out her arms to them. She remains suspended between silence and crying out. Between life and death. Between the path and the wine-press. Between the figs and the grapes. She isn't saying anything. She doesn't know how to speak. She won't speak. She can't speak. Except to the lizard who comes to see her once in a while. Except to the cauldron that François heats up. Except to the blanket once in a while. She has an illness. She doesn't know what it is. Denial? Distress? Hope? François in the fields every day. The first daughter taking care of the house. Silence. The silence of the child. The silence of François. The silence of Victorine. Language impossible to break. Language which can't express brokeness. She can't speak French. Too many words are missing. How can one tell the misfortune of

servants. Servage? How can one express despair. Servitude?
How can one express nostalgia. Servance? How can one say
murder? Servation? How can one say state? Servement?
No. They say subservience. They add more action and lose
the pain. They have to dominate. They have to master.
They have to separate. Action or state of being, never
both. Separation. Never separement. How will I express
what they have done so badly? Separage? What hurts me
so much. Separance? What hurts us so much? Separatude?
The action or the state, never both. The tearing. Never the
tearation. How can one know the source of the tearage?
How can one speak the evil of the tearance? How give
witness to the tearitude? She can't. She stays in bed. She's
paralysed. She won't speak French. She wants no part of a
crippled language that only says half of everything. She
wants no part of a language that forces a choice between
the murderer and the murdered.

The silence of François. The silence of the little girl
who is escaping with him into the fields. She doesn't want
to stay locked up. She wants to see the trees and the
mountains. The road between the cemetery and the castle.
The road between the figs and the grapes. The road
between the water and the land. The race to get back to
François. It's February, time to prune the vines. It's February, time to get back to François. The twigs. The fire-
wood. The fire. It will be February for some years to
come.

Victorine is ill. She's sick of staying in bed. She's sick of
living and dying. She's sick of all this pain. She's can't
speak French. She remembers. She's not sure just what.

She dares not remember any more. She stays in bed. Paralysed. Mute. Suspended.

She's suspended on the Wheel of Fortune. She can only move if someone spins it. They say this is an illness. They don't know what it is. They don't know the two animals clinging there. One goes up. The other comes down. They don't know the sphinx at the top of the Wheel. They say she has an illness. They don't know what it is. Intermittence. Fusion plunging down. Separation coming up. The tranquil sphinx on high. The reunion of fusion and separation. Love. Knowledge. No. They say it's an illness.

The first daughter does the cooking. Victorine stays in bed. She's not crying. Not laughing. Not speaking. She's waiting for François to return. She has an illness. The breaking. Strength broken. For months. For weeks. For years. Sick for love of the frogs and the meadows. For her father's house. For the blueberries and the raspberries. For the stones and the insects.

They say this can't last. Something's going to happen. She doesn't yet know they have condemned her. She doesn't know it's death she must guard. She doesn't know she's guarding death so that they might live. She doesn't know she's their safeguard. All she knows is that she can't speak.

The waiting in bed. Life in suspension. A coffin. A garden with two trees. The tree of life. The tree of knowledge. Perhaps it's only a house. Or the arms of François. Or the belly of Victorine. Perhaps it's the love of François and his wife. Or the flight of their daughter through the vineyard. How can one know? How is it possible to remember in this crushing oppression of my life? How is it possible to remember in this tearing apart? Something has happened. What? I don't know. A love story. A murder. A curse. What was it?

If I could remember, I would find the three-year-old woman. I would find again this woman whose hands are all I know of her. You say I know her. That I have already recognised her. That she's waiting for me on the path. That she stayed right where I left her. That she has been waiting for me for thirty thousand years.

They say they must lock her up so she will protect them. They say they're going to lock her up so she will save them from the water. She lives in the wash-house. She makes their life impossible. She opens the floodgates of the canals. Unleashes the fountains. Floods the gardens. They say if she dies they won't get wet any more. She's the reason the wash doesn't dry. The rivers overflow. The stones sob. The ravens laugh. She smothers infants. She causes miscarriages. She eats children. She's the daughter of the night. She lives in the marshland. She carries off the dead in her cloak. She buries them in her belly. She keeps alive the memory of all that has come about. She waltzes across the plain with her black horses. No one can look on her without dying. Men are afraid because they can't name her.

What happened to this three-year-old woman? What have they done to her? Why did I abandon her? Why have I gone on without her? What has become of her? You know. You won't tell me. You say I must continue up the path. That I'm halfway there. That soon I will find her. You know what happened. You have always known. I'm on my way to see you in order to learn what happened. You say that it's not worth the trouble since I know already. You say I've always known and that's the reason I'm coming to see you.

The path continues. Increasingly narrow. Increasingly hard. More and more isolated. So much love. So much time. So much love and time to find this woman. Who is she? How does it happen that all I can see are her severed fingers? What are they playing? What are they playing with their miserable cards? They're playing skip my turn. They're playing at pretending to believe that I'm not part of their game.

Here now is Strength on the path. She has a blue dress and a red cloak. She wears a headdress. She holds a lion by her side. She holds a lion's jaws open. A lion's jaws open with nothing but her two hands. She holds a lion's jaws open. He won't be able to bite. They won't be able to bite any more. Something has to happen. A denouement. A safeguard. A return to water. A solution.

Is this my life? Waiting. Intermittence. Dependency. Love. They keep me because I protect them. I protect them because I'm dead. Maybe not completely. Otherwise how could I be waiting for the return of François? Is this my life between the bed and the wall? Between death and rebirth? Between fusion and separation? Waiting for the reunion. The illness. The suffering. The separance. The oppression.

The oppression of all these dead women before me. The oppression of this line of mad women. From mother to daughter. From grandmother to granddaughter until the memory of it is lost. Right down to the oldest one among us. Right down to the little girl of three. Until she says: I consent. Until the one who consents to die rather than kill. The sickness all day. The separance. The suffering. A lineage of mad women. Casting the evil off on one another. Thinking they're rid of it. Until the smallest, the oldest says: I consent and will protect all the others.

Consent. Consent to being their thing. Their object. Their reject. Their little reject. Their offspring for a new birth. A death and a rebirth each day. A death and a rebirth closer and closer together. Until they pulverise time and space between their hands. A death and a rebirth so close together that their hands open up to reunite what they have separated. So close that she becomes her own opposite in a time before time, in a place before place, in the primordial chaos of the womb of the world. The oppression of this line of mad women, from mother to daughter, casting the night off on one another and losing the day, until the maddest one among them gathers up all their madness, saying: It belongs to me.

Victorine is waiting, lying on her bed. Victorine waits all day. Every day. So what is she waiting for? If she knew, she couldn't do it. If she knew, she'd run away. If she knew, she couldn't consent. Victorine is waitng for the murderer.

I don't want to. I'm running. Running. Running. But they're on my trail. They're running after me. I see their arms ready to suffocate me. Their teeth to devour me. Their hands to silence me. I'm running up the path. I'm running toward the three-year-old woman. We're running together toward the river. You stay seated in your big chair. Your hands are moving. Victorine doesn't move at all anymore. She's waiting for us in her bed.

Where are these words off to in search of disaster? Where are these words going, seeking the murderer? If they knew, they wouldn't go. Where are these hands going in search of the lost woman? If they knew, they'd stop writing. What are they going to look for, these hands that don't even belong to me? What are they seeking that is so essential it makes them invade my entire life? What are they looking for that is so tragic? What are they going to look for all by themselves? What they have always known. What they pretended to forget.

Where are these hands off to? They're going in search of death. The fourth of this name. The one which overturns. The one that moves toward life. That of copper: possession. It's nothing. The deaths of the brain. I've known so many of them. The first of lead. The second of pewter. The third of iron. Of all these deaths, I prefer the fourth. That of copper. Because it's the one before the first.

You're looking at me with your severed fingers. You're saying if you wish, we will be reborn together. Through you we will remember. Because of you we won't die. She stays stretched out on her bed. The little girl is running in the vineyard. The little girl runs to François. Victorine can no longer bear the pain of love. The wash-houses. The reeds. The birds. She can no longer bear remembering. The waterweed. The damp wash. The flooded garden. She can't bear the water in her body, in her head, in her life, any longer.

You're saying that if only you could walk you'd die happy. If I hold out my hand to you, you will be able to get up. If I believe it, it will happen and she won't die. If you hold out your hand to me the frogs and the reeds will return. If I hold out my hand to you we will return together to the country of the marshlands. You've kept the memory to be able to pass it on to me. Looking at your hands you say it's time. All you say is the fingers of the fig-tree. You're laughing. You don't know what that means anymore.

Victorine waits at home in bed. Victorine waits for love to impart the memory. The frogs. The wash-houses. The marshlands. But language? Language won't. Language can't. Language can't convey all this water. Victorine can't speak French. She won't speak French. She only knows one language. The one they didn't teach her. She stays in bed. She's sick with love. She won't be cured. Love sickness can only be cured by love itself. She can't speak. Because of the language. How to tell the love of the murderer and the one murdered? How to say being together self and the other? How to say action and state of being? How to say separation and fusion? Day and night? Earth and water? How to say the contrary without saying the negation? Victorine is ill. They don't know what she has. She's ill from speech. She's ill from separation. She's ill from the creation of the world.

They say she's ill. That she can't be cured. That she will never be cured. That is the fourth death. That of copper. Of tiny bells around the ewe's neck. Copper kettle on the stove. Of bells on the fool's cap. The fourth death. The death of the possessed. The possession. She can't be cured. The language can't be reunited.

There's the woman in mauve showing herself off. There's the madness-maker ploughing my brain with her nails. Ploughing the soil of my disaster to sow the seeds of

madness. Raking the paths of my love to tear out everything that grows. Sprinkling the seeds of destruction with
poison as she laughingly casts them about. Pruning the
plum-trees to make orchards beyond reason. Making cut-
tings of the oak-tree of knowledge so I won't recognise it.
Sawing the tree of life in the garden of my obstinacy.
Instilling poison into my flowering trees and attacking my
newly burgeoning fruit. Grafting death on my consenting
trees. There she is, the one who cries: Jeanne is mad. Jeanne
will die. Jeanne belongs to me. She's laughing at my
despair. She's sure of her victory. She digs in my head to
extract my spirit. She sits at table in my skull to suck any
living juices. She aspirates everything that moves. She
squeezes drop by drop the lemon of disparagement. She
sniffs out any remains in the middle of the pile of corpses.
She's the queen of jackals feeding on dead meat. She's the
madness-maker who thinks she's living by destroying.
She's hunting me down in the walls of the house. In her
hands are the fragments of my cerebral flesh. On her head,
the trophy of my tree of life. She tans my cortex to make
a drum beating out the call to her courtiers. She trims her
mauve veils with the membranes of my brain. Her pearls
with my medulla. Her necklaces with my cerebellum. She
sniffs around in my skull for anything that might still be
alive. Nothing more.

My brain is a pile of stones. An overturned ruin. A
wrecked house. My mouth is the silent portico where
unsaddled black horses are galloping. The earth has
trembled. For the fourth time. The fourth death of the
brain. The death of copper. The bracelets. The basins. The
cauldrons. The fourth death. The gardens are open graves.

The cities in ruins. The rivers dried up. She runs after me laughing. I hear her singing: Jeanne will die. Jeanne is mad. Jeanne belongs to me.

There's the stone mountain with no birds or insects. The mountain that shelters the city of the dead. The mountain of overturned stones. I'm fleeing over this desolate pyramid. I'm running, I'm running up the ascending path. No one's here anymore. This is the death crossed so many times that I know it by name. It's the fourth. That of the convulsed women. The crazed women. The possessed women. The death of those who don't know how to separate: possession.

I'm running toward the stone mountain. The mountain constructed by stuttering hands. The pyramid formed by a gestating world. The mountain one crosses to get to the other country. The land of the wine-press. The garden of the two trees. The oak and the birch. It's the road to the fig-tree. It's where the regiment of words cross in search of the murderer. There Victorine is waiting for the return of François. There Victorine is sick from love. You wait upstairs in your wicker chair. You have a red dress and a blue cloak. You're holding a book between your severed fingers. You have a veil on the back of your head. You're guarding the passage. You're guarding the border of the country of the living. You devour those who want knowledge without experience.

This is the city of the dead. The dwelling of the woman in mauve. She has a castle near the lake. There she feeds the birds. She's following me. She's holding you prisoner. This is the red river that must be crossed to look for the three-year-old woman. What happened to her? What have they done about it? Where have I lost her? For all the many years that I have been on the way to meet her. The many years they have been keeping me from getting to her. The many years they have held her prisoner. Where is she, this woman of three? She's on the other side of your veil. In my rejoined hands. In my severed fingers. In your withered hands. Where is she, this woman of three? You say she was a witness to the murder. If I find her she'll talk about it. If I find her, I'll recognise her. She's there where the regiment of words crosses over.

I'm running. I'm running up the path. But they're on my trail. They don't want me to escape. They don't want me to live. They say I'm going to die. That I must die. That I like dying. They're teaching me death. They want it. They say if I don't die they won't be able to live. They cast death on me so they won't have it with them. I'm their emissary. Carrying the message they don't want to the separated country.

I don't want any part of it. I'm running to escape them. The woman in mauve is with them. She's crying out. Death to the mad escapee. Death to the companion of the serpents. Death to the daughter of the birds. Death to the living woman.

They're going to catch me. I'm fleeing among the fallen stones. My feet torn. My hands bleeding. I'm fleeing into the mountain. She's laughing. She says they'll catch up with me. Because of the three-year-old woman. Because of the little woman I haven't forgotten. Because of the one living by the river bank. She used to love the trees and clothing made of fern leaves. I'm fleeing but I'm not running fast enough. The little girl calls me. I recognise her voice in the shortcomings of the language. The woman of three holds out her arms to me. She says take me away. Where is she under all these fallen stones? Where is she under all these destroyed joys? Where is she under all these forbidden desires? Where is she in this country of death? Where is the little girl who waits for me?

The physical struggle with death. The physical struggle with suffering. Every day. Well, not quite. Once in a while, a respite. Because of François' hands. Because of François. Because of François' laughter. Once in a while a respite. The fields and the forests. The raspberries and the cherries. A respite. Just barely. Just enough to keep from dying completely. Just enough to keep on running. Just enough to escape them a bit longer. Just enough to go and die a bit further on.

The physical struggle with death. The daily suffering. The steel lung of words. The physical struggle with a body that doesn't belong to me. The physical struggle to find the woman lost for so many years. To find the lover of raspberries. To find a body to give to these hands. To find again the mouth of this woman whose name they have changed. This necessary woman. Lost for so many years. The woman from the time before the separation. From before the possession. Before the appropriation. She so loved life. Wild strawberries. Toads in the wash-house. The shacks in the bushes. The three-year-old woman. My eldest sister. My youngest sister. My little girl. They took her. They imprisoned her. What has happened? What happened the first time?

They were running up the path after her. She was running. She was fleeing. She had seen something. What?

She saw something on the path. She runs into the mountain of stone. They're after her. What was it she saw that explains death? What did she see that gave her entry into the night? Whatever was it that she saw? No, she doesn't know any more. She won't remember anything any more. She will die. Whatever did she see? A thousand suns. A thousand suns with only one name for all of them.

She has seen the Hanged Man on the tree of the murderer. She has seen the Hanged Man upside down. On top of the stone mountain. In the middle of the road. She saw the Hanged Man in front of her wicker chair. She saw the Hanged Man in front of Victorine's bed. She saw the Hanged Man and she ran toward them. They were pursuing her. She ran toward the ones who were shouting death. She fell the first time. The three-year-old woman. She fell in their midst. She has seen the Hanged Man. She can't live any longer. She fell in their midst. For such a long time she has been running. Such a long time she has been escaping them. Such a long time they've been pursuing her. They caught her at the top of the mountain. You watched them do it. You watched them catch her to take her away. You watched them with your severed fingers. She lay down on the ground in their midst. On top of the mountain. They caught her. She consented. They gave her a name. The woman in mauve was with them. She bent over the convulsed body. She leaned toward the three-year-old woman. And she said: 'Oh look, she's like Victorine.'

She recognised me. She doesn't want me. How could I know that? How could I believe it? How could I? I open my arms to her. The curse. Heredity. She recognised her.

She knows her, the one walled up in the wine-press. She recognised me. She doesn't want me. She doesn't love me. An hereditary illness. What is it then? Consent? Memory? Love? She recognised me. She doesn't want me. Since the beginning it is the beginning of the night. I hold out my arms to her. But hers don't open. Her body doesn't open. Her belly doesn't open. She corrects my mistakes in grammar. My love. My irrational love. My love against all reason. My promised land. My fertile valley. Not so. She doesn't want me. It's night. The red death. The wash rinsed in the wash-houses of my brain. Endless death. Rejection. Exclusion. Emission.

In the garden the spirit gives an order to man saying: of every tree in the garden you shall eat, but of the tree of the knowledge of good and evil you shall not eat, for from the day that you eat of it, of death you shall die.

But they eat of it anyway. Because of wisdom. Because of love. They eat. They make love. They know. They find union of opposites again. Death and life reunited. They know fusion and separation. They discover that they are naked. They can't bear it. They prefer to separate from each other. They hide in the tree of the garden. They sew leaves from the fig-tree to make girdles for themselves. They need a scapegoat. They can't look without losing strength. They hide the truth from each other.

Man says to the spirit: the woman you gave to be with me, she gave me of the tree. I ate. And the woman in her turn said: the serpent seduced me. I ate.

They know good and evil. They know fusion and separation. But they prefer to separate. They exclude themselves from the original garden. They have eaten from the tree. But they forbid themselves the tree of life. They're afraid. They can't bear knowledge. They're going to lock it up.

A garden with two trees. Knowledge and life. But they can't bear it. They exclude themselves from it. Two trees and a third one as well. The tree of the murderer. They take it with them. They take it along in their girdle. To separate it. To curse it. To wither it. To lay on it the burden they are unable to bear. They carry it along to guard death. They are going away to the orient. They are going toward life. Her name is the Living One.

They will invent farming. They will have three sons. The first to die. The second to be dead. And the third to forget. They will be father and mother of the murderer. She will name her first son: I Have Acquired. He will be the first blacksmith. They will dominate the world. They will live because of the tree they are carrying with them. They will live. I won't.

I hear the woman. I hear her every day. She's walking by the lake. I hear her parasol and her mauve veils. She's the mother of the murderer. I hear her singing. Jeanne is cursed. Jeanne is separated. Jeanne will kill herself. She's laughing. She's coming to see me in the depths of my torment. She's coming to see me to torment me still more.

Victorine the night. Victorine the frogs. Victorine the wash-houses. The broken body. Stiffened legs. Hands spread wide. Victorine the convulsed body. The rebellious hands. The lost language. Victorine sick with love. The little girl of thirty thousand years. The three-year-old woman. Victorine trying to give witness with her body. In her body. In spite of her body. Victorine trying to say. What exactly? What the language can't express. Possession. Denomination. Appropriation. Victorine trying to say power. Trying to resist power. Trying to survive power. Victorine seeking a way to say. The other thing. The other place. The other world. Victorine of the night. How could she? What language can recount the murder? What language can say the separation? What language can say the suffering of the separated? What language can say the ignorance of the separator?

Victorine of the marshlands. Of the reeds. Of the birds. Victorine of the edge of the river. What happened? A murder. A murder in the mountain. A murder on the path. A murder in the fields. A murder in the middle of the card game. A murder in the beginning of the world. A murder in order to live. The consent to murder. Whatever for? By what impossibility of living? What memory passed on? What acid crossing through the brain? What molecule coming along with life? What happened?

A murder at the end of days. The murdering one brings fruits of the earth as an offering to the spirit. The battered one also bringing the oldest of his flock and their fat. The spirit accepts the battered one and his offering. The murdering one and his offering, he does not accept. The murdering one becomes very angry. He is downcast. Why are you downcast? The Spirit says to the mudering one: Why get angry? Whether or not you can tolerate it, the fault is laid at your door. It is you she desires. Will you govern her? The murdering one says to the murdered one, his brother... And it's when they are in the field. The murderer rises up against his brother. He kills him.

What happened? A murder. Consent to the murder. On the mountain path. In the fields. The murderer rises up against his brother and kills him. He separates the chaff from the wheat. He separates the winnowed grain. He has name I Have Acquired. He has separated.

It's nothing. It's only a murder. The initial murder. The murder without which life isn't possible. The murder of the uprooting from death. The murder after the creation of the world. The murderer rises up against his brother and kills him. He has name I Have Acquired. He's the first separator. He's the first blacksmith. He takes power. He kills half of himself. He locks up what he can't appropriate. I Have Acquired rises up against his brother the Winnowed and kills him. He locks up what he can't name. He locks up opposites gathered together. He locks up the unnameable.

The spirit says to the the murderer: Where is your brother who has been killed? He says: I don't know. Am I my brother's keeper? He says: What have you done? The voice of your brother's blood cries out to me from the earth and now you are cursed by the earth which has opened its mouth to take the blood of your brother from your own hand. When you till the soil it will not put forth its gift of strength to you. You will be unstable and a fugitive on earth.

The murderer says to the spirit: My wrong is too great to bear. Yes, today you send me from the face of the earth. Could I hide from your face? I am unstable and a fugitive on earth: whoever finds me will kill me.

No, the murderer can't die. He has name I Have Acquired. He is alive. He is named. He is separated. He is cursed. The spirit says to him: Every killer of a murderer will suffer vengeance seven times. The spirit marks the murderer with a sign. No one on finding him will strike him.

The sign on the brow. The mark of the stone. The sign of blood. The wound of the murder. The murderer can't die. Without his murder he can't live. He has a mark on his brow. That of the red acids. It's nothing. It's the curse. The separation. The murder. Becoming mad. Withering. The wine-press. The separation of the figs and the grapes. Of the dead and the living. Of water and land. Of wet and dry. Reason locking up half of itself. Reason killing half of itself in order to live.

The murderer goes out, far from the face of the spirit. He inhabits the nomad's land in the Orient. The land of the living. The land of ignorance. The land of innocence. The land of unknowing. The land of opposites, not of negation. This is the drying up. Separation encompassing contraration. The worm stinging the tree of the murderer. The tree. The tree in the garden. The tree of the murderer. The tree that gave him shade. The tree that comforted his pain. The tree withers. In one night. The night of the murder. The tree gives no more shade. The tree makes no more separation. Now she is the separation.

– Oh look, she is like Victorine.

The murder. Murder in the body. In order to live. To separate. To exist. The tearing of the bird's wing. The stick on the serpent's back. The hook in the mouth of the fish. The first step towards life. The murder impossible to commit. The murder without which life is impossible. The woman in mauve is laughing and singing. Jeanne can't live. Jeanne belongs to me. Jeanne will die. The woman in mauve in the meadow. At the lakeside. In the marshlands. She has a sign on her brow. The mark of a stone. She has a sign on her brow. That of the murderer.

What are François and the little girl playing? What are they playing with their poor little game? In their hands I'm the deadest of cards. The one that has a place and no name. What is it they're playing? If they knew, they couldn't. They're playing at pretending to believe I will survive. Pretending to believe I can still live. They're playing at continuing to live. At proposing I should live. So many games I don't know the rules of. How could I play with them? I don't know how to separate. I'm both cards and hand together. Table and wrist. Carpet and bench.

This is the other side of the mirror. The Arcana Without Name. The land of the Unnameable. The land one can't cross without dying. How can one say the contrary without expressing negation? How can one talk about crossing over outside of one's self? How can one say death for rebirth?

You say it isn't true. That they haven't been able to catch her. That she didn't fall. That she managed to escape. That she went between two trees. That she passed right under the Hanged Man. That she went to another country. That she fled. That she crossed through the mirror. You say she's living. That she's running in the mountains. They can't kill her because she has a sign on her brow.

If I were Victorine, they would not have let me go. But they didn't let me go. I ran away. I ran away while they were on their way to get me. No. When they caught me. Because they did catch me. I escaped between the vines.

Up the path behind the village. I ran away toward the shepherds. I ran away through the wash-house.

If I were Victorine, they wouldn't have let me go. But they pursued me. They pursued me and I ran. They pursued me. The woman in mauve was with them. And she was shouting: Jeanne is mad. Jeanne belongs to me. Jeanne will die. She was shouting and she had a stone in her hand.

If I were Victorine, François would have brought the rhubarb from the garden. The rhubarb from his little garden. The rhubarb from under the withered tree. He put it down on the corner of the table. But it's no use. I can't get up because of that run up the mountain. That run up the path. That run in their card game. Because of the raspberries and the periwinkles. The wash-house and the frogs. The grasses and the moss. The cat on the wall. The laughter of the child. The anemones. The buttercups. Because of the love sickness.

How does it happen that I remember the time before the illness? Before becoming mad. Before the curse. Before the creation of the world. Before the murderer. Before the withered tree. The time when I was able to live. The time when you were able to live. The time when you were walking. The time when we used to run in the stream. How is it that I have kept the memory? It's because of that tree between earth and sky. That withered tree. It's the tree of the murderer. It marks the border of the separated countries. You say it mustn't be torn out otherwise the whole country will dry up. How is it that I remember as well the time afterward? The tree was planted to save the living. It dried up to protect the whole village. It dried up so there would be no more separation. It took death upon itself.

This suffering. A testimony. A passion. No. A love. Nothing but a love. This suffering flesh and blood. Verb and word. The impossibility of living. The impossibility of dying. Consent. The body drowning, sinking every day. Hands reaching out to the blue barque of the ferryman. Hands reaching out to you with my severed fingers. The impossibility of living. The impossibility of dying. The living stone. The withered tree that gives no shade. The tree no longer causing separation. The cursed tree. The tree with the severed fingers. The tree outside of time. The tree of eternity. The tree nothing can bring to bloom. The tree that guards death. The tree of the murderer. He's dead. He's alive.

They say that dead and alive can't be said at the same time. Their language can't say the contrary without saying the negation. That is the language of the separators.

The language of the separators can't say the contrary without expressing negation. Death, not non-life. It can't express negation without saying the contrary. The non-madness, not the cure. Their power rests on this confusion. Their power depends on this denial of contraration. They forget one half of reason. They forget what they've locked up. They forget her whom they have killed. They say any old thing. That I confuse identity and difference. But that's exactly it, difference is identity. They say that's the sign of my illness. If only I had been able to learn. I would be able to explain to them. But no. Her stern look. The metallic clink of the ruler on the table. I'm bored. I do everything they want me to do. I sit in the first row. I answer all their questions. I answer what they want me to. I'm bored. Nothing to do. I always confuse identity and difference. Thesis. Antithesis. Synthesis. I forget. Thesis. Antithesis. Synthesis. If I had learned. Now I'd be able to say to them: Thesis. Antithesis. Synthesis. I'm bored. The metallic clink of the ruler on the table. Her stern look. Our grey school smocks all alike. Stop. I hurt. I'll never amount to anything. I confuse identity and difference. Thesis. Antithesis. Synthesis. They aren't able to conceive of con-traration. They say contradiction and they get lost. How can you say to them Land. Water. Land-Water. How can you tell them that they're forgetting the marshlands?

I'm dying of it. I died of it. The metallic clink of the ruler on the table. Her stern look. Can do better. Jeanne Hyvrard can do better! Has knowledge but doesn't work hard enough. I don't understand. I don't understand what they want. Can do better! Can do better! So many years spent crossing death. Surviving death. Surviving in death. Can do better! I don't understand what they want. Can do better? So many years spent not confusing death and non-life. So many years spent resisting the rolling mill. So many years spent refusing the three mad women thesis antithesis the two siamese and their daughter synthesis. Grimacing. Deformed. Synthesis who had all the fairies at her bedside. Reason. Possession. Finesse. Mastery. Deformed synthesis. Grimacing. Walking with a crutch. Synthesis, little daughter of error and lies. How can they put back together what they have separated?

So many years the tree with the withered hands. The tree in the middle of Victorine's garden. The tree that gives no shade. The tree that separates no more. The tree all alone like an island in the flooded garden.

I'm running up the path. I'm running to get away from her. She's shouting. Come back. Come back. Remember when we used to play together. Remember. Hopscotch. The river. The pink quilt. She opens her arms to me. I run to them. Is she the little girl of three? Is she the one I've found again? Is she the one who grew up? Of course, I'm the one. How could I not love you, my mad little one. Why wouldn't I love you? You're going to die soon.

I'm running to get away from her. I'm running over the stones. I'm running up the path. This is the second slope of the mountain. The ascending one. She can't catch me. She shouts. Come back. Remember. Hopscotch. The ferns. The ravines. But she's pretending. Just to catch me. She's not the one, the little girl. It's a trap.

I'm running up the ascending path. I'm running to get away from her. Here's Temperance. I know her. I've seen her so many times. She has a red dress and a blue cloak. She has two wings and two vases to decant the water. She pours one into the other. She says I mustn't run and I must stay in bed. Otherwise the earth will dry up. She says I must stay in bed because of all the water she's pouring from one vase into the other, without spilling a drop. She says I must stay in bed and it's my turn to guard death.

That's the woman in mauve near my bed. The woman in mauve at the head of my bed. The woman in mauve standing near me. The woman in mauve decanting death without spilling a drop.

– Oh look, she's like Victorine.

François can't nourish his three daughters. He leaves in the morning, his stomach hollow. Victorine waits for his return. Victorine the simple. Victorine and her three daughters. She stays in bed. For weeks. Months. Years. Paralysis. Mutism. Despair. Denial. She's stiff. She says nothing. The first daughter keeps house, cooks and serves the meals. The first daughter destined to die. Victorine doesn't move. She waits for the return of François. The return of her love. The return of the man. They say she can't go on like this. She has an illness. They don't know what it is. Love-sickness. She hurts in the frogs. In the wash-house. In the reeds. In the strawberries hidden under the leaves. The cherries in the trees. In the grass brought to the rabbits. The vegetable peelings. The dog in his box. The velvet cushion. The laughter. The periwinkles. She hurts all over. They say she has an illness. They don't know what it is. Separance.

Suffering. The hurt of tearing. The hurt of morning. The hurt of the bodies tearing themselves out of the night. The hurt of the bodies rediscovering the day. The hurt of being torn from François. The hurt of arms unknotted. She has an illness. Love. The body of François. His hollow stomach. His body of lilacs. His body of love. His body of silence. His body of hands. His body of arms. His body of mouth. The reunion of night. The reunion of sleep. The reunion of the bed.

François can't feed his three daughters. The first one destined to keep house. The second to run in the vineyards. The third to stay home. François can't feed his three daughters. He leaves in the morning, his stomach hollow.

In the evening he comes home tired. He sits by the side of the bed. He holds her hand. He says nothing. He doesn't know how to talk. Mute, he keeps her company. He carries his cauldron on a very long journey. He doesn't speak. She doesn't speak. How could they? Neither the one nor the other knows how to speak French.

The first daughter is going to leave. She's leaving for the city. Exile. Exodus. Deportation. She leaves the fields and the meadows. The rivers and the wash-house. Apple -trees and hazel-nut trees. She's leaving her family for the city. The buildings. The streets. The first daughter goes off.

François leaves in the morning, his stomach hollow and returns in the evening tired out. The second daughter also goes away. Jeanne the exile. Jeanne the exodus. Jeanne the deportation. She leaves the fields and the meadows. The rivers and the wash-house. Apple-trees and meadows. She leaves her family for the city. The buildings. The streets. She goes away. Carrying away the memory. She goes away to be dead.

I stay in bed. My two daughters have gone. The first to die. The second to be dead. The first to be a servant. The second to be a servant also. They have both left. The first, the mother of the dead woman, and the second who was her own daughter. They both went away. And the third one too in order to forget. The third one to lose her name.

The red acids are dripping. This is the city they have assigned to be my dwelling-place. I know the walls. These are the panes of glass and the mirrors that sparkle. They tear my body apart. So many acids rise up the river of the heart of summer. An uncrossable river. A river that must be crossed however. I know it. It's the one that flows between my withered hands.

I know the city of the dead. It's in the shadow of my brow. Thought bursts as it passes through the mirror. Pain crushing my temples. But I have only to consent to put an end to the suffering. I have only to consent to the death of the brain. Blindness. Mutism. Deafness. Paralysis. I have only to consent to hurt no more. This is the fifth death. The death of the red acids. The death of mercury: Acceptance.

Death lasting for years. The wine-press. The city of the dead. The death-house. The surge of red acids drowning the love of life. It's nothing. It's death coming. One mustn't cry. She has a mauve dress and a sunshade. I know her by name. I have seen her passing through the meadow so many times. This is the hour of renunciation. Consent to death in order to get through it. Death-ment. The death of the brain. The crematory oven.

This is the house inhabited by the laughter of ravens. They peck at my eyes but they can't dim the light. They squawk but they can't muffle the song of the world. They nest in my skull but they can't kill the spirit. Even in the midst of its opposite. In the midst of suffering. In the midst of loss. In the midst of the brain dying. Companions of red acids. Don't cry at the laughing of the ravens. It's only death passing. Don't be afraid. It opens the world's body. It opens to totality. It opens to knowledge. We are guarding the memory of the earth.

So much fatigue and suffering. A storm at sea wrecking my poor ships. A storm. A storm of red acids. Not to resist. To go to bed. To let it pass. To stop thinking. To stop searching. To stop struggling. To abandon yourself to death to get through it. The red waves are surging in my brain. They carry me away. They bear me farther off. They disappear if they don't meet with obstacles. The red acids are dissolved in absence. This is a poison secreted by thought. One must let the water run. It will carry away the blood. It will become clear again in the wash-houses of the mind.

Temperance tells me to stay in bed. She pours me from vase to vase. She pours me without losing anything. She transmutes me. I will not die since I am already dead. I will not die because of the red acids.

The complaint of the mind torn from the order of things. The complaint of the mind subjected to an order not its own. The red acids distilling death. The red acids protesting in the crucible of the cranium. The red liqueur in the alchemist's oven. The uniting of sulphur and mercury. Paralysis. Death. Eternity. The return to the time before. The effort of thought to separate the inseparable. To give direction to chaos. To dominate opposites. To master the order of things. To order time. To orient space. To resist death. Confusion. Sinking. Erosion. Being swallowed up. Thought striving toward life. Thought striving toward separation. Striving to separate things from their opposites. Striving to refuse death. Man emerging.

Fatigue. The complaint of the brain violated. Waste from effort. The red acids, thought tearing itself from the order of opposites. Reason fracturing contraration. Reason fracturing oppositation. The red acids becoming more and more dense until they paralyse thought, forcing it to return to chaos. To the time before. To the place before place. To the time before the separation of light and fusion. To the time before the separation of day and night. The return to the time of chaos. The seventh day. Fallow land. The repose of the earth. The ransom of the domination of agriculture over stock farming. Of the murderer over the murdered one. Of power over identity. Of the real over the imaginary. Of action over being. Contrariness. Not negation.

The deaths of the brain, I know five of them. The first of lead: resignation. The second of pewter: submission. The third of iron: oppression. The fourth of copper: possession. The fifth of mercury: acceptance.

The red acids to escape from them. I'm running up the path. They follow me. They throw stones at me. They're going to catch me. They're going to wall me up in the wine-press. They shout death to the escapee. I'm running up the paths. I'm running in the vineyards. I'm running toward the fig-tree. The woman in mauve is with them. She says: Jeanne is ill. Jeanne will be cured if she takes care of herself. Jeanne can be cured if she wants to. I run. But the three-year-old woman holds her arms out to me. The three-year-old woman says: Take me along. Because of her, I'm not running fast enough. Because of her, I can't get away. Because of her, they're going to catch me.

I'm running up the path. There's the Devil rising up out of the bush. Rising up from disaster. Rising up from suffering. Rising up out of the red acids. He says I can get well if I want to. The Devil says he has the remedy. He says: If you wish it, you will suffer no longer. He's half man. Half goat. Half man. Half woman. He's the Devil.

The bearer of light. The divider. He has several names so as not to be recognised. He has two arms. One to solidify. The other to dissolve. He's the one who says: Choose. If you wish, you will suffer no longer.

The deaths of the brain, I know five of them. And the fifth one especially, the one that can be cured. The fifth. The death of the Devil. The death of those who so wish can be cured. The fifth, that of temptation. Of the evil one. Of the serpent.

They say they have remedies. Medicines. Drugs. They say I can be cured. They think they know but they refuse to know. They want only to make us like them, confusing contrary with negation. They want to cure us. Of what? They invent our illnesses to make us forget. They invent our symptoms to cool our ardour. They invent remedies to silence us. They want to cure us of what finally? Of obstinacy? Of refusal? Of fidelity?

They want to know in order to act. To correct. To regulate. They want to know in order to have power. They say they have drugs, medicines, remedies. But they don't know the red acids. The liqueur of mercury. Of cinnabar. The sign of blood on the forehead of the murderer. The sign that reunites the murderer and the murdered one. They say they have remedies. We don't want any of them. We have on our forehead the sign of eternity. The red acids of death and rebirth. The gold of the alchemists. The philosopher's stone. Memory.

They say they have remedies. But they don't know the red acids. One day they will separate them. They will name them. They will fabricate them. One day they will possess them. They will know the land you live in. The cause of your consent. The chemistry of the drama. They will establish the formula of the red death. The matter of the stone of madness: the molecule of memory. They will know the why of love. There'll be no going back to the bosom of opposites. No more return to the time before. No more death. No more rebirth. They will be completely separated. Their power will be total. They will be alone.

The deaths of the brain, I know five of them. That of lead. That of pewter. That of iron. That of copper. The deaths of the brain, I know five of them. The fifth the most terrible. The one from which one can be cured. That of mercury. Of the red acids: acceptance.

The Devil says I can be cured. But how will I find what I'm looking for? Without the red acids, how will I find the thirty-thousand-year-old little girl? How will I find the three-year-old woman? How will I recognise you, you who are waiting for me in your wicker chair? How will I reunite what they have separated?

How will I find the lost language? The lost words. The molten words. The words transmuted in the great cauldron. The hollow of language. Contrary, not negation. This illness they give so many names to. Except his. The memory of life.

Divide. Separate. Analyse. Oppose. Or. Or. Or. Never and. Death or life. Love or hate. You or I. Or. Or. Or. The real or the imaginary. Action or state. The sacred or the profane. The body or the mind. The humid or the dry. Or. Or. Or. Never and. Reason locked up can no longer bear it. She rebels in the corridor of those condemned to death. Or. Or. Or. Never and. Reason rebels. She wants no more separation. She wants no more of what they've taught her.

She wants to jump the fences to run in the fields. She wants the stones for crossing the rivers. She wants raspberries to help her find her way. Learned-thought rebels. Reason bangs against the wall. Thought no longer functions. Reason transmits information. Thought is no longer operative. Reason communicates through separation. The supervisors panic. They call the guard. They sound the alarm. Divide. Separate. Command. Or. Or. Or. Or. The great cry of the supervisors in the corridors of those condemned to death. But they can't maintain order any longer. Reason locked up communicates by knocking on the walls. And. And. And. And. And. Death and life. Love and hate. You and I. Power and identity. The real and the imaginary. Action and state. The red acids cross through the walls of reasoning. Fracturing the mirror of reflection. Going through cell doors. Seeping from all the pores of the brain. The guard can no longer stop reunification. Opposites opposed rejoin by going through the walls. Offended opposites are recovered in the red acids. Opposites dismayed are reinscribed in the order of things. The order of reunification. The order of contraration. The order of death.

I'm running up the path. They're after me. They want to cure me. They shout let's cure the mad woman. The woman in mauve is with them. She shouts louder than they do. She shouts Jeanne is mad. But Jeanne will be cured. Jeanne will die. She shouts louder than they do. She has a lace dress and a parasol.

I run. So hard. So fast. So far. There's the Tower in the middle of the road. The tower struck down. The crown overturned. Pride decapitated. One must continue to run.

The tower is overturned because it was blocking the road. The tower is overturned in order to continue moving forward. You have a red dress and a blue cloak. You are in the wicker chair. You're holding a book. You have a veil on the back of your head. You're saying one can't know. You're saying that if I walk I will find her. You're saying if I walk I will recognise you.

You're saying that one can't know. One can only bear witness. To memory. To life. To separation. To withered language. To senseless sense. To misleading voices. You say one can't know. One can only bear witness. I'm running up the path. They're after me. They want my death in order to silence me.

I run toward the mountain. I run from fatigue. From exhaustion. From despair. I'm running through all the dead. I know so many of them, these women form a cradle for me. I know so many that by holding hands these women get me across. I know so many of them that they keep me alive. They watch over me as a sick dead woman. They guard me with so much care, my five mothers. The first of lead: Resignation. The second of pewter: Submission. The third of iron: Oppression. The fourth of copper: Possession. The fifth of mercury: Acceptance. All their mothers bringing forth all the others. They watch over me, all these deaths, so no one can touch me. They are all around me. They protect me. They have mauve dresses and lace. They have parasols. They sing all around me. They sing: Jeanne is mad. Jeanne can't live. Jeanne will die. They sing all around me so no one can come near me. So no one can take me away. So no one can kill me. The red death and her four daughters: Resignation. Submission. Oppression.

Possession. The red death and her four daughters. They have put upon me a sign so the living will not carry me off. I belong to them I'm with them. I'm from them. I'm in their cauldron. Matter in fusion. Across all sufferings. All decomposition. All transmutations. I'm their work. Their Great Work. Their Philosopher's Stone.

The deaths of the brain. I know so many of them that I can no longer die. I'm like these women. Drowned in the red river. Burned in the acid. Charred in the refractory earth. Those men want to cure me. I'll have none of it. I'm running up the path. I'm running to escape them. I'm running so fast I can't go on from exhaustion. I'm going to fall. I'm going to cry out. They're pursuing me. The woman in mauve is with them. She tells them: She's mad. Catch her. Cure her. They're on my trail. They want to lock me up in the wine-press. They run after me. They throw stones at me. I run to escape them. I don't want to be cured. I want to find the language they have mutilated. The path gets more and more rugged. Narrower and narrower. I'm hurt. My feet hurt. My hands hurt. My head hurts. My writing is hurting. My whole body hurts. I hear them laughing derisively. The woman in mauve shouts: Stop. Stop, Jeanne. You're going to die of fatigue.

You watch me run. You say: Don't look back and you will recognise her. You point her out with your severed fingers. You point her out and you say don't look at her. Don't pronounce her name. Don't call her. You move your poor withered hands. You move your paralysed body. You say, if only I could get up. I reach out to you. You say: Don't look at me and you will recognise me. You have a red dress and a blue cloak. A crown. And a wicker chair.

You have a book in your severed fingers and a veil on the back of your head. You say: Don't turn around and you will recognise me.

You show me the top of the mountain in the depths of the river. You say: Run and you will recognise her. Run and you will recognise me. I'm running to the limit of my endurance. Across words. Evening and morning. Again at night in dreams. I'm running through fields of verbs. Meadows of adjectives. Wash-houses of nouns. I'm running, climbing over all they have separated. Through sentences gasping for breath. Across words that escape me. In search of the beginning. Seeking the language spoken by the ravens.

The path ascends. A lake. There's the dwelling-place of the woman in mauve. That's where she lives. There she holds you prisoner. There she feeds the birds. This is mountainous country. The country I come from. The country where you are. The country she dwells in. The land of motionless suns. The land of chaos. The land from before the separation.

This is the land of Stars. There is a naked woman beside the lake. A woman on her knees with two urns. In her left hand a silver urn. To pour water over the land. To moisten the earth. To make the earth fertile. In her right hand a golden urn. To pour water into water. To pour boiling water into dead water. A naked woman beside the lake. A woman pouring water from the two urns. She's the same one who decants from one vase to the other. It's the same water not a drop of which has been lost. The same water she pours over the earth and over the water. The same water. The boiling and the cold. The urns of gold and silver. The right and the left. The naked woman is on her knees beside the lake. There is an acacia branch to hide a tomb. To disclose a death. There is a plundered flower. How can there be so many stars?

There are stars to be the well-spring of tears. The well -spring of water. The well-spring of memory. There are so many stars that they change night into day. So many stars they bear witness to the middle of the night. So many stars that they are seven. Four and three. Death and life. Right and left. Gold and silver. They are seven. Four and three. And the eighth one as well. The shepherd's. The brilliant one. The double one. The last one. The first one. Memory. The unity of opposites. Love. Right above the naked woman. Right above the urns. The eighth star. The double one. The unique one. The union of opposites, to shine so brilliantly that it makes one think of day in the middle of the night.

I'm running up the path. I'm running toward that star. I'm running to the lake. Toward memory. Toward love. Toward fusion. Toward confusion. I don't know if identity means alike or difference. I'm not sure any more. I fuse and confuse with more and more force. Faster and faster. More and more things in the huge cauldron. The woman in mauve is pursuing me. They are pursuing me. They're with her. They're running to catch up with me. She cries out to them: Jeanne must die so that we may live.

They want to subject me to the order they invent. To the order of the murderer. To the order of creation. To the order of separation. They want me to become like them. They force me to repeat: Two times one, two. I'm bored. Her stern look. The metallic clink of the ruler against the table. Two times one, two. No. She's mistaken. Two times one: one. The clink of the ruler against the table. Two times two: four. No. Two times two: one. Her stern look. I'm bored. Jeanne Hyvrard can do better! Years of mistakes in arithmetic. Years of mistakes in addition. Years spent resisting the separators. Can do better. They divide me. I multiply myself. They add me up. I subtract myself. I disappear. I'm bored. The metallic clink of the ruler against the table. Two times one: one. Our grey school smocks all alike. Our names embroidered. Two times one: one.

François is sleeping in the morning light. François is sleeping in the song of the birds. François is sleeping in the insects and the grasses. Summer will soon be here.

Victorine can't live or die. Victorine the tearing apart. Victorine the junction. Victorine the night. The doctors say she is ill. They don't know what she has. They say only that she can't get better.

François leaves in the morning, his stomach hollow. The daughters have left. The first to die. The second to be dead. The third to forget. The daughters have gone to the other country. To the city. To the factory. The daughters have gone to another land. To the country of the dying.

The daughters have gone. Not one is left. No one comes to the wash-house anymore. No one comes to see Victorine. They have gone to serve the masters. They have left home. The maids. The kitchen girls. The servants. They've gone. There's no one any more. Only the lizard. And François who doesn't talk. François cultivates. François sows. François harvests. François washes her. François dresses her. François rocks her. François loves her. François thinks she's going to survive.

Victorine sees the withered tree through the window. The cursed fig-tree. The tree of the murderer. The tree of I Have Acquired. The named tree. The separated tree. She watches it through the window. She resembles it. They gave her to guard what they don't want. What they can't bear. What they reject in fusion. What they refuse: contraration. The order of contraries. The order of death. They have given her to guard what must be separated in order to live: memory. She's the separated one. The cast-off one. The rejected one. The guardian of the way. The one who was sent. She's dying of it.

I don't want to. I don't want to guard what they give me to guard. I don't want to stay in bed. I don't want to be the tree of the murderer. Their cover. Their protection. Their emissary. I don't want them to lock up in me the contraration that goes contrary to their domination. Their nomination. Their power. I don't want them to cure me of the illness they invent for me. I don't want to play the role they attribute to me. I don't want to protect them from what they disown.

I'm running up the path. I run with so many words, I'm going to escape them. They're on my trail. The woman in mauve is with them. She cries out. She shouts louder than they do: Jeanne belongs to us. Jeanne will die. Jeanne must die since she guards death. I don't want to. I want no part of the death they are inculcating into me for want of being able to live with it themselves. I don't want to guard death. I don't want to be cured.

I'm running up the path. You say, don't turn around. Above all don't turn around. Your arms move. You point to something that I can't see yet. Something behind your veil. You're seated in your wicker chair. You have a red dress and a blue cloak. You're holding a book in your hand. You tell me: Above all don't turn around. Run, run and you will find the thirty-thousand-year-old little girl. The three-year-old woman. The necessary woman. The woman of words. The woman of the severed fingers. The woman they are pursuing. You say they haven't walled her up in the wine-press. That she wasn't from around here. That she came from somewhere else. That she left again. That they weren't able to kill her. You're moving. You move more and more. You are not completely paralysed. Maybe it would be enough for me to say one word for you to stand up. Maybe it would be enough if I call you by your name. It's the name of the unnameable. How shall I pronounce it?

You are going to get up. One word is enough. We're going to go in search of her. She's not far off. She's in the death-house by the lake. She's seated in her chair. She's waiting for us. At a sign we will recognise her. You tell me: Run! Run without turning around and you will recognise her.

I'm running up the path. Day and night. Evening and morning. I run through language that has been stabbed through. It keeps me from living and from dying. I'm nothing but a body resisting the brazier. A bellow of words firing up my own funeral pyre. The hand of death mowing down the oat field of despair. The hand of death wilting the meadow of lost happiness. The sickle of writing harvesting disaster. The wicker basket of phrases recollecting forgotten memory.

I'm the defoliated land. The diverted river. The polluted sea. The ploughed countryside. The enclosed meadows. The devastated fields. I'm the land they are trying to take over. They build bridges. Dig tunnels. Change climates. Cross plants. Kill species. They dominate the world. They monstrefy our dwelling. But they will never succeed in drying me up.

They can't dry me up because my hands don't belong to me. They belong to all of us. They can't dry me up. I live outside myself. I live in language. I live in all that has ever been and in all that will ever be. I am part of all. I'm a part of all of each part. I'm part of all that is coming and over coming. I am part of all that is living and surviving. Because of these hands. These hands rising up again. These hands that are the servants of words. They are the servants of memory. They are my two daughters. The first to die and the other to be dead. These hands of a lost body. The body of hazel-nut and raspberries. The body of stones damming the river. The body of toads in the wash-house. Hands from the time before. The hands they left me. Hands to hold out. Hands to bear witness. Hands to write. Hands that are nothing but words anymore. Hands that are the only things left to me from happy times. Hands with fingers severed so I can neither reunite nor separate.

They can't dry me up because of the red acids. So many pass that death itself can't get through any more. So many pass that the order of things is disordered by them. Opposites are opposed. Sense is insensed. The way is wayward. So many red acids pass that they deposit their alluvium on the stones in the river. The red death in the depths of my brain. The waste from combustion. The residue from the decanting. Accumulated death. It buries the river. Muddies thought. Silts up memory. Death to be cleaned up. Death to be washed. Death to be put to death. So many red acids pass through that one must begin again. The moment of execution. Alcohol. The explosive mixture. The ritual murder. Alcohol to drag the bottom of the brain. Acid plus alcohol. What unknown mixture? Acid plus alcohol. If I had at least learned chemistry.

No. They say I'll never amount to anything. All I know of chemistry is the clink of the ruler against the table. Her white lab coat. Her stern look. The musty odour of cupboards. The coloured crystals in big glass jars. The white laboratory bench covered with test tubes. The black nozzle for the gas. She looks at me sternly. She doesn't like me. All I know of chemistry is the big red and black chart. The letters of the elements. The letters of the names of the elements of the earth. All I know of chemistry is the dreams of mingled bodies. Copper and oxygen tarnishing the chandeliers. Chlorine and potassium scrubbing the sink. I know nothing of the chart of elements except the title of my dreams. The periodic classification of the elements. Reds and blacks. Reds and whites. The lines. The columns. The letters. The numbers. They have left empty boxes for the dreams gathered on the roadways. The metallic clink of the ruler against the table. Her stern look. Her glasses. She doesn't like me. Classification of the elements. They have forgotten the red acids. The hands of the trees. The veil of the woman in mauve. She says I mix everything up. She's right. Periodic classification of the elements. All the treasures of our bodies neatly in order. But some boxes escape them. The empty ones. I'm living in them. I'm bored. Our grey school smocks all alike. Her white lab coat. Her stern look. The metallic clink of the ruler against the table. She's going to send me outside again. Periodic classification of the elements. The red acids are missing from it. Maybe not. If I had been able to learn chemistry. No. I'm not learning anything. I pretend. If I remembered at least. I would have less pain now. But no. I don't remember anything. Or barely. Or so little. One thing only. The red acids perforating my life of distress. The red acids constantly throwing happiness back into the chaos from before the creation of the world. If only she hadn't had that stern look. Her glasses. Her white lab coat. A single memory. Suffering: acid plus alcohol... Acid plus alcohol? Today's suffering. No, she didn't like chemistry. Nor the pupils. Nor the bodies. She didn't like anything. Her stern look. Her white lab coat. Her coldness. Boredom. The metallic clink of the ruler. I don't understand anything. I'm not learning anything. Acid plus alcohol. The red acids. Suffering crossing the empty squares on their charts.

They say I don't know anything about chemistry. They're right. I know only the acids when they turn into horses in the mirror. I'm not learning anything. She wants me to repeat with her: acid plus alcohol equals... No, I don't know anymore. Acid plus alcohol? I can't retain it. I only see the sky through the window. I hear the lament of the wood in the desk. Acid plus alcohol? Our gray school smocks all alike. Our grey school smocks with our names embroidered. I'll never get anywhere. Acid plus alcohol?

I'm bored. The metallic clink of the ruler. The inkpot tipped over on the white page. The smock torn on the iron rod. Acid plus alcohol? The black horses beyond reason. Acid plus alcohol? The esterification of my disaster. Acid plus alcohol gives ether plus water. The reaction is slow and limited. It's reversible. They say I can be cured.

Acid plus alcohol? Execution. What beverage to give courage? What ritual to get past death? I'm the expiatory victim of my own disaster. The emissary between the two worlds. Acid plus alcohol. The reaction is slow and limited. Acid plus alchohol. The paroxysm. No, not completely. Intoxication. Coma. Not yet total destruction. The organ music of death. Rage. Ravage. The broken dishes. The torn clothes. The burned papers. The cracked mirrors. Acid plus alcohol. The sixth death. The death of silver. Despair. End. No, not completely. The reaction is limited. It's only the sixth death. Liquification. Solution. Liquidation. The deaths of the brain. I know six. The first of lead: resignation. The second of pewter: submission. The third of iron: oppression. The fourth of copper: possession. The fifth of mercury: acceptance. The sixth of silver: fusion. Death invading the whole brain. The red death connecting all the cells. The red death. The sixth to return to chaos. Acid plus alcohol gives ether plus water. This is the beginning of the rain.

This is the downpour over the land. Forty days and forty nights. The waters swell and abound over the land. They cover the mountains under the heavens. And everything that has breath breathes life in its nostrils, all that is on dry land dies. It's the deluge. The fortieth by name.

The one before the first. This is death crossed over one more time. The sixth, that of silver. Of liquidation. Of fusion. The raven flies off. The waters cover the whole earth. Contraration covers affirmation. The return to the belly of the world. The return to the order of the world. Fusion. Opposites reassembled. Water covering the earth. Unlivable. It's nothing. It's only death passing by. The sixth. The fortieth. The one before the first. Which ark holds reason? In whose hands is reason enclosed? By what cover is reason protected? By what pitch? By what sap? By what resin? By what missing word? By what substance missing from the tree of the murderer? By what substance absent from the one that is withered? What substance without which life is not possible? Self love? Safe keeping? Hermeticity ?

It's nothing. It's the sixth death. The deluge. The return to the bosom of opposites. The rain of disorder forty days and forty nights. Floating in the ark of the arms. The wood of memory carrying off rebirth along with it. The birds of contradiction. The reptiles of confirmation. Ancestors of them all, the fish of interrogation. Carrying them away two by two male and female. Separating and fusing. The dove seeking food in vain. The deluge. The death of silver. The sixth. The return to the time before. The origin. The debut of the species. The time from before the separators. From before the domination. From before the nomination. From before the murder of the murderer. The time from before I Have Acquired and his brother The Winnowed. The return. The fortieth. The time before the first. The dawn of the species. The return to the marshlands. The womb of thought. The body of the mother, not separating self and the other. The effort of reason trying to survive unreason.

The sixth death. That of silver. Fusion. Death dealt by ourselves. For ourselves. To ourselves. We destroy ourselves rather than destroy our destroyers. Rather than ignore our desiccators. Rather than separate our separators. We turn death against ourselves. Greedily. Eating greedily. Drinking deeply. Racing madly. Speaking volumes. Breathing deeply into a coma. Howling. The great organ music of death in our upset bodies. Cantatas of destruction. The debacle. Madness turned against us rather than separating.

The flood washing the accumulation of red acids. The body cast into the water to be reborn. The body from the crematorium to be resurrected. My metal body melted in the alchemist's crucible. For what transmutation? For what transformation? For what new alloy? For what new alliance? My body of words melted down for what disaster? For what memory? For what knowledge? For what rebirth constantly beginning again in the depths of the waters? Life given back to each consented death. To each death passed beyond. To each death passed over.

Life given back by this shoreless crossing. By this perpetual shipwreck. By this body renouncing life. Life given back by way of the game. Life given back in the path that passes between their hands. Life given back each time I can't play. Each time I can only say: Pass, in the midst of their shuffled cards. By what hand that always puts the Queen of Swords and her sister the woman in mauve in my hand? By what hand that constantly shuffles the cards in the game, always giving me the same cards. I never have a winning hand. I'm always the one who deals death. Because of what game inscribed in the nucleus of my cells? Because of what transmitted memory? Because of what connection in my neurons? An illness? Rejection? Love? An hereditary illness? Stubbornness?

I'm running under the Moon. To the end of my strength. Toward the marshland of lost memory. Toward contraration. Toward the time from before. There was a swamp. But the path goes on. Heading toward the horizon. It passes beyond the horizon. Toward a solitary night. Toward a still more tragic night. Toward a dark night. One must pass between the two towers. One must pass between the two dogs. One must pass to get through. They're on my trail. They pursue me to the edge of the marshland. They pursue me under the Moon. There's a crayfish. Or a crab. Or a cancer. There's a crayfish in the swamp. The path goes on. Or no, rather. The path leaves the marshland. The path is swallowed up in the night. The path is swallowed up in the distance. One must get past the two dogs. They're howling under the Moon. They are called Conservation and Procreation. One must get past the two dogs and the two towers. One must must get past the two powers of the world and move forward into the night. The path sets out into the most deserted of deserts. There are no more stars under the Moon. Nor eyes nor light. Nor flowers nor woods. There's no longer anywhere to take refuge. One must keep walking.

They're following me. They're on my trail. The woman in mauve is with them. She's singing: Jeanne is ours. Jeanne belongs to us. Jeanne will die. Look, she's not defending herself. It's nothing. It's the passage. One must cross between the two dogs. One must cross to enter the night.

This fatigue. This illness I don't want. This illness they have given me to bear. This illness they have taught me. They're pursuing me up the path. But they won't catch up with me. I'm running so fast. I'm running so far. I'm outstripping them. Not completely. They're after me. They shout death to the escapee! Death to the runaway! Death to the dead woman! The woman in mauve is with them. I recognise her. We have been playing together forever. Together we play the role they taught me.

But I'm not playing anymore. I pick up a stone on the path. I pick up a stone to hit her on the forehead. I pick up a stone to break her head. She has a dress made of lace and ribbons. I recognise her. We have been playing together forever. She can't die unless I die myself. She leans toward me. She sneers. She kicks away my clutching hand. My hand reaching toward the living. My hand reaching toward the sun. She's nothing but her mauve dress. She is nothing but this laughter and this parasol. This derision. This unreason. She laughs at my monstrous body. At my stiff arms. At my immobile mouth. She steps on my hands to make me let go. She laughs. At my charred head. At my body in the shifting sands. At my eyes pecked by the ravens. At my mouth gagged by the toads. How is it that I don't die? It's because I hear the tinkling of the oats. They're following me up the path. But they won't be able to catch up to me. They're blinding me but I am the echo of the lakes. They're drying up my body but I'm the moaning of the road. They're burning my brain but I'm the sizzling of the stones. How is it that I don't die? It's because of the laughter of the woman in mauve. It can't fracture the unity of the world.

They're pursuing me but they won't catch up with me. Because of their din. It's not loud enough to cover the minute pulsing at the heart of things. Because of their lie. It's not thick enough to mask the light of the stars. Because of their resignation. It's not empty enough to deceive the body of love. Because of the laughter of this woman. This is opposition, not negation.

Pain ravaging my head to make it a home for birds. Suffering to exhaustion. Suffering stubbornly pulverising my skull. The suffering of bombed-out land. The impossibility of capitulating. Fields beaten down. Trees defoliated. Houses razed. The terror of the living amid the howling of words. The countryside sacked. The disaster of the molehills. Earth words now and then. A gallery of animals terrorised at the sound of steps. A path for a body in such misery that it can't turn aside. A tunnel for hands digging in the night. A subterranean life under an abandoned culture. One last relay before the end.

They're pursuing me up the path. I'm running in brambles. Through brush. Up the path. They pursue me. The woman in mauve is with them. She shouts: Jeanne must guard death so we may live. Jeanne will die.

So many trees. Raspberries. Cherries. So many stones on the path. One has only to pick one up. A single one. The thinnest. The weakest. The most fragile. Disarmed and invincible. Dead and incorruptible. Abandoned and living. It fits in the hollow of her hand. It plugs up the hole in her palm. It makes the separation. It is the writing.

I will drown without this pain in my forehead. The bruise. The spot of blood. The blossom of the poppy on the stone. The lady bird in the grass. The raspberry in the palm of the hand. The bruise. Mortalitude. The mark of the stone. The sign of the murderer to stop the murderer. The stone of the wall. The stone of the body. The stone of suffering. The stone of the revolt. The stone of survival. The stone of the murder.

A stone so small that it's part of the hand. It can't hold on to anything. It makes fusion and separation together. It came from the mouth of the volcano. So that one might gravely engrave on it gravity and gravitation. One has only to pick it up and throw it at them. This stone is all one needs to be able to live. The stone of the murder. The unnameable. The unpronounceable sound. The sound lost naming the world. The beginning of writing. The period.

The stone on the path. The stone picked up among the vines. The stone picked up under the fig-tree. The stone of necessity. The stone of the tearing apart. The stone of the joining. The stone that separates the murderer and the murdered one. The stone that reunites the murderer and the murdered one. The writing. My fault is too great to be born. Anyone who finds me will kill me.

No. Whoever kills the murderer seven times will be subject to vengeance. The murderer strikes his brow. The murderer beats his brow. The murderer bruises his brow. He puts a sign on himself.

It's nothing. It's only the seventh death. The death of gold. The last. The one before the first. The only one that counts. The death of gold. The end. The abandonment.

The crossing of the lake. The blue barque of the boatman. The voyage made only once. It's nothing. It's death approaching. Having passed by so many times, here it is finally crossing me. Having seen it pass by so many times, here it is finally stopping. This is the end of hope. The end of the love of life. The separated country. The end of the voyage. The beginning. The laying bare. The ending. The last stone between the two towers. The stone of the walling-up. The stone of the crossing. The last stone cementing the night. The death of gold. The seventh. Abandonment.

One must pass between the two dogs. They are called Procreation and Conservation. One must pass between the two towers under the Moon. That's where one crosses over. The stone in the depths of the water. The laying bare. The ending. The seventh death. The death of gold. Reason pierced. Body in the brazier. Body abandoned. Head against the walls. Screaming. Life torn apart. Body on tenterhooks. The whole body in darkness. Blindness. Deafness. Walling-up. The last ties broken. The woman in mauve sings: Look at the mad woman. She's bruising herself. Her body abandoned to the fury of the walls. Her flesh torn by the daughters of the divider, escapees from the stones. The women walled-up tearing out my eyes with my own nails. The women walled-up piercing my ears with my own cries. The women walled-up tearing my mouth with my own words. Violence crushing its own revolt. The unleashing of the forces of darkness. The body submerged in its own pain. The whole body using all its strength to destroy itself. The whole body organising its defeat. The whole body busy killing itself. Contortions. Convulsions. Screams. The laughter of the woman in

mauve. She's waiting. She's singing this time she will die.
She's right. When they are in the fields. The murderer rises
up against himself. And he kills himself. The death of
gold. Confusion.

The path continues. It's no longer worth the trouble to
run. They won't be able to catch up with me. Because of
the dark night. The last light has gone out. The other world
is in this one. The passage is a two-way mirror. That's
where one crosses between the two dogs. Conservation
and Procreation.

They think I'm going to die of not being able to tell
about the passage. The action and the state. The murderer
and the murdered. The possessor and the possessed. They
think I'm going to die of not being able to say the separance because they have only kept the separation. They
think I won't be able to say separage, separitude, separement, separals. They think I won't be able to tell of the
thousand pains of the separated ones through the two-way
mirror. But I will break language into so many pieces that
it will reconstitute itself. Into so much debris that there
will be enough for every wound. Into so many shards that
it will finally reflect the light of motionless suns. They
think I will die for not being able to say action and state
together. Subject and object. Word and wound. Discourse
and suffering. Separation and separement. They are mistaken. I will say separity.

I'm coming to see you in the death-house. By the lake.
In the castle of the woman in mauve. I'm coming to see
you following the path. I recognised you in your wicker
chair. By your withered hands. By your severed fingers.

I'm going to call you by your name. I have always known it. We have only one name for all of us. I caress your withered hands in my hands from another time. They are the hands of the three-year-old woman. The hands of the thousand-year-old little girl. The hands of the necessary woman. The hands of the lost woman.

I have recognised you. I love you. You are going to get up. You're going to begin walking again. Perhaps you never really stopped. Perhaps you're the one running up the path? Perhaps you're the one who crosses between the two dogs. Conservation and Procreation? Perhaps I'm the procreated one? Perhaps I'm your daughter? Or your mother? Perhaps we have the same grandmother? The lost little girl. The same grandmother who waits in bed for the return of François.

We have the same grandmother and the same daughter. The one who runs up the path. In the desert. In the night. The same grandmother and the same daughter. They pursue her. They're going to wall her up in the wine-press. Her fingers are severed. She stays in bed. She waits for the return of François. The path continues in the dark night.

The impossibility of being in separation. Of remaining separated from the world. Of being outside the world. Of existing. Inexistence. I'm going to survive because of this inexistence. The opposite of necessity. The opposite and not the negation. The opposite of necessity. Not existence. Essity.

The Sun at the end of night. The Sun above the wall. Lighting up the wall. Reuniting the two sides of the wall. The couple. The man and the woman on the carpet of flowers. The man and the woman in a wreath of flowers. The man and the woman under the Sun. The man and the woman in front of the wall.

I am under the Sun in the wreath of flowers. I have no identity. I am separation and fusion. I'm nothing but the infinitive of the verb which means both to live and to die. I'm nothing but a pronoun which calls you and me together. I and she. Us and me. The indefinite pronoun. The infinite pronoun. The pronoun of unity. The noun of the unnameable.

They oppose separation and fusion. As if these were not the two children in the wreath of flowers. As if this were not the couple under the Sun. As if this were not the couple behind the wall. Of which house? Of which death-house? Of which wine-press? The couple against the wall under the Sun. One by the other. One towards the other. The same body. Guarding the whole in their parts. The separators and the separated. Those who wall up and the walled-up. The murderers and the murdered ones. The living and the dead.

They separate power and identity. Action and state. The real and the imaginary. They oppose the two parts of the world so as not to recognise them as one. Because they would have to question the unnameable. And they can't bear his silence.

Death is coming soon. My death soon. Just a short time to walk up the path. Just a short moment to get to see you in the death-house. You tell me don't turn around and you will find her. But how to leave her in bed, this thirty-thousand-year-old little girl? The three-year-old woman. The necessary woman with the withered hands? The woman with the severed fingers? How to leave her. Every day she waits for the return of François. He leaves with his stomach hollow. He returns tired out. Sometimes he plays with the child. He plays cards with her. He plays cards along the path. He plays cards without looking at her.

She may be the one pursuing me up the path. She may be the one keeping me from getting up. She may be the one on the pathway. She may be the necessary woman they want to wall up. She may be the one crying out: Jeanne is mad. Jeanne is mine. Jeanne will die.

I walk up the path. Until my strength is spent. The end will soon be here. The wine-press. The death-house. The hospital. Soon that will be all they want. Judgement. The mountains of the separated country. The mountains of the living. The mountains of home. A herald with a big trumpet. A herald to announce what really? The end and the beginning. Death and rebirth. The new age. The end of death. The new language. Speech. I'm under herald's trumpet. The man and the woman at the tombside. Fusion and separation. And the child of both of them. Alloy. Alliance. Love. Their child whom they can't name. Unity.

I'm holding you in your wicker chair. You are moving your stiff legs. Because of this alliance. This maternity. This reunion. You are going to walk because of your name the unnameable. Because of our love. Because of our finding each other again. You are going to walk. I have pronounced your name. I have called you by your name. By the name of our love. By the name of the living. I pull you out of your chair. You get up finally. You walk.

After so many years of waiting. So many years of

paralysis. So many years of death. You are my accursed granddaughter. My paralysed granddaughter. My separated granddaughter. My granddaughter older than the earth. My granddaughter bearing the memory. You're walking. They haven't killed you completely. They have only shut you in. But I recognised you by a sign. By your withered hands. By your hands which can neither reunite nor separate. By your hands of eternity.

I am the laundress of the night. The woman they want no part of. The first. The ogress. The vampire. The dragon. The owl. The octopus. The crab woman. The cancer woman. The crayfish woman. The first woman of the first man. I come out of the crucible of the alchemist. In the blood of the women. In the red acids. I come back in all that is red. The belly of the figs. Painted mouths. Polished nails. Abysses. Chasms. Caverns. I come back in all that is hollow and bottomless.

I am the womb of night. The mouth of volcanoes. The desire of fissures. The mother of birds. I stifle children in gestation. I digest foetuses dead from hunger. I regestate the bodies buried in my belly. I don't know how to melt metals. Nor classify numbers. Nor order space. I know neither grammar. Nor arithmetic. Nor chemistry. I am disorder. Unreason. Confusion. I'm the first woman of the first man. The one he can't look upon without dying.

I'm the first woman of the first man. The one whose name he has forgotten. Drawn from the silt of the earth with him. His equal. His companion. His deliverance. The one who didn't eat the fruit because it was her own belly. The one who didn't seek to find out since she already knew.

The one who was not expelled since she hasn't separated.

I'm the first woman of the first man. He separated another from his side. In order to subject her. So she would obey him. So she would mask the half of the world that he can't bear. He separates another from his side in order to be excluded from the original garden with her. To conjure me he calls her the Living One. But he can't forget me. I am his memory. His remorse. His bruise. I'm his first wife. His deliverance.

I'm the sterile one. The thirty-thousand-year-old little girl. The three-year-old woman. The rebel against the creator. The runaway they have pursued all the way to the sea but whom they haven't been able to catch. The rebel against the creation. The first woman of the first man. I come back at night to haunt his dreams and in his dreams we reach out to each other. I am his loved one. His friend. His comrade. The one who loves him and doesn't want to obey him. The one who wants to inhabit the whole earth with him. The one who holds out her arms to him to get to the country of the living. Not the one who ate the fruit. Not the one who said: The serpent tempted me, I ate of it. Not the one who rejects what she can't carry. Not the one who can't look without weakening. Not the one who needs an emissary to be taken care of. Not the one whom they call the Living One. Not the mother of the murderer. The other, the first woman of the first man. The red one.

I am death passing through decimated streets. Let them put their dead in my cart. I take them all. The dead from indifference and the dead from despair. The dead from preference and the dead from regrets. The dead from vengeance and the dead by chance. I take them all, these dead who are encumbering them. I take them all. And we go. They and I. Alike. Reunited. I guard them on my endless journey. In my drowning without a harbour. In my grape harvest without wine. I keep everything they don't want. I guard everything they refuse. I give witness to everything.

They say I speak a language they don't understand. But they hear it all the same. Because of the brazier. It's the language of midnight. The first hour. The smallest. The longest. The hour of morning. The first hour of the world. The language forbidden in schools. The language forgotten from mother to daughter. The language transmitted from grandmother to granddaughter. In the skeins of wool. In the pans of the kitchen. In the laundry of the wash-houses. The language of the night. The language of the body. The language of the fig-tree disfigured by the raisins of reasoning.

They say they don't understand her. But they hear her all the same. She has crossed all the deaths. The first: resignation. The second: submission. The third: oppression. The fourth: possession. The fifth: acceptance. The sixth: fusion. The seventh: confusion. She has crossed all the deaths as far as reunion. They don't understand the language of the fig-tree. But they hear it all the same. They hear the part and the whole together. The body a member of the world's body.

They're pursuing me up the path. They think I'll die of not being able to say things and their opposites together. They think I'll die of not being able to say separation and union. But I will say the hand. Consent and suffering. I will tell the tree of the murderer. Knowledge and misfortune. I will tell her withered hands. Death and rebirth. I will tell the women's bellies.

They're pursuing me up the path. They think I'll die for not being able to say together body, reason and spirit. They think I will die for not being able to reunite what they have separated. They are forgetting the language of the fig-tree. They don't understand it. But they hear it all the same. I will say together, death and life. Contraration, fusion, the sacred, the madness, the unlivable. I will say water. I will say together, affirmation, reasonableness, the profane, the livable. I will say earth. Earth and water. Reasonableness and folly. Profane and sacred. I will say the earth that unites them. I will say the water that unites them. I will say earth and water. And their love, the marsh-lands. The tearing apart. The joining. The memory of the waterweed that lives there. The reeds of writing. The birds who guard them. The birds of passage. The birds of con-tradiction. Of treachery. Of mediation. Birds of love. Birds of death. Serpents too. Serpents of life. Of confirmation. Of temptation. Of wisdom. I will say the love of the birds and the serpents. And the ancestors of both the fish. The fish of questioning living in contraration. The fish dying in the reasonableness of affirmation.

They believe I'll die of not being able to say the separa-tion. But I will tell of first morning. The creation of the world. Genesis. We invented death thinking we could contain it. We invented death and we're afraid of it. We shouldn't have separated it.

They say they don't understand the forgotten language. But they hear it all the same. The language that says everything and its opposite. The language that reunites everything that must not be separated. The language from before language. The language of the body. The language of the world. The language we speak without knowing it. The language of the separators transmitting in spite of themselves the memory they want to destroy. Language showing the way to those who seek it. Hiding it from those who fear it. Separating the moist from the dry for those who don't want to get wet. Hermetic language. Language that reassembles everything they have separated. Language of symbols. Language that is its own opposite. Language that separates and reassembles. Unique language. Every day language.

I'm coming to see you in the death-house. You tell me what I've always known. You tell me about the body crushed by impossible forgetfulness. Legs paralysed by refusal. Fingers severed by the memory of the time before. You tell me what I've always known. The love of Victorine and François. The wash-houses. The frogs. The reeds.

They've come to get her to wall her up in the wine-press. She saw them coming. She heard them coming. She watched them come. Since she was already dead she couldn't run away. That's why they chose her. They came looking for her to take her to the wine-press. She didn't defend herself.

She preferred dying to being separated. That's why they chose her. To be the tree of the murderer. The tree with no protection. The withered tree. The tree that gives no shade. The tree possessed. The tree of I Have Acquired. She took separation upon herself. To bring about the joining.

They came to get her and you accompanied her. She didn't cry. She consented. All she said to you was: The fingers of the fig-tree. Nobody knows what that means and that's why it must be repeated. So it won't be lost. Until it is understood. Until it is remembered. Until it is found again.

They came looking for her to wall her up in the wine-press. They came looking for her to wall her up in the death-house. She didn't defend herself. When the last light went out, she kept walking, guided by the hum of insects coming from everywhere. She had a mauve dress and a parasol. She showed you her hands and her fingers were severed.

The earth was afraid and it trembled. The earth was hurting and it cracked open. The earth got angry and erupted. So many stones and so many words that the birds fled from the rocks. Toads invaded houses. Hands engraved epitaphs. Springs dried up. Walls wailed. But that wasn't enough. The murderer didn't want to remember. He threw the stone of the crime into the garbage dump. He has name I Have Acquired. He is alive.

We're going home. You and I. We have crossed over walls to find each other. We're going back to our house. In the country of valleys higher than mountains. The country of lakes. Frogs. Wash-houses. We're going back home. Victorine is waiting for us. You and I. I and she. All three of us. We're walking toward the country of the high lands. Mother and daughter ourselves. For such a long time.

I come looking for you in the death-house. We will go together to find the protector. You become tiny again in the blue belly of the ship. You become tiny again in the cradle of my arms. So small and so light. You are so old. So withered. You have no more flesh. No more sap. No more pitch. No more resin. You are nothing but a dead leaf on the tree of the murderer.

I will take you out of your wicker chair. I will carry you like the cloak one wears to the ball. The cloak on my monstrous shoulder. The cloak of splendour. I will open my blue and gold wings and it is your name they will see tatooed on my flesh. We will look for the lover of frogs. The daughter of the wash-houses. The laundress of the night. We will go together to get her. We will arrive one day at noon. In radiant sunlight. We will come one day at midnight bright as day. I will carry you small and light. I will come through the gates. The park. The walls. I will come in my carriage of waterweed rolling over the sand. We will keep going until we reach her.

I'll say I'm coming to get her. I will steal her away, the deceased from her iron tomb. I will steal her away, the mummy of memory. I will steal her away the dead one of the motionless suns.

We will return to our home in the mountain lakes. In the reeds where the swans nest when they brood over their enormous eggs. Near the banks. By the side of the pasture land. In the barques of the morning. We will survive. We will lay the dead woman out in her mauve adornments. We will lay her out on a bed of velvet. We'll keep her parasol. We'll return home crossing the lake. We'll return to find our houses destroyed and our fields abandoned. We'll return to the time without verbs and sentences without pronouns.

Don't be afraid. We're going to find her. She has been

waiting for us since the leaves of the hazel-nut trees. Since
the day of the raspberries. Since the dams in the streams.
She has been waiting forever. Since the Hanged Man on
the murderer's tree. Since the first scream. Since the curse.
Since the separation. Since withered hands. Since severed
fingers. Since open arms.

Let's go and find her. Let's go and find her to bring her
home. We're going to meet her. The cypresses. The path.
The wild grasses. The high walls. The barbed wire. The
portal. The butterflies. The park. The path through the
trees. The benches. The ditches. That's where she's holding
her prisoner. That's her castle. She has been waiting so
many years for us. She's singing. Do you hear her? She's
singing: Jeanne will die. Jeanne will not have a child. Jeanne
is excluded. Don't be afraid. She can't do anything to us
anymore. We have found her again. We are the daughters
of one another. We're coming to get her. The trees. The
leaves. The dovecote. Death behind the walls. The dry-
ness. The scorched leaves. Summer and winter alike.
Death. The immobility of time. Space suspended. The
benches. The path through the trees. The castle. The basins
of the fountains. The flowers. The stairs. The death-house.
The wine-press. The hospital. The cypresses. The walls.
The portal. The reunion of space and time.

Don't be afraid. We're going to find her. She's singing
under her parasol. She's singing with her lace. Don't be
afraid. She can't do anything to us anymore. We have
found each other again. You have always been with me. We
have only one body. Only one mouth. A single cry. Only
one life being walled up.

Don't be afraid. We're going to find her. The steps. The

basins of the fountains. The stairs. The corridors. The bed.
The bedroom. The mattress. Don't be afraid. She's no
longer here. It's too late. She's gone. They say she has left.
Gone still farther away. That she wasn't from around here.
That she returned to her country. That she went back
across the ford of motionless summer. They say they
pursued her. But they weren't able to catch up with her.

She's no longer here. She lives in another country. High
on a hill. Your withered hands. Your severed fingers. The
way you looked before. My vacant eyes. My mouth gagged.
The body broken by the love of life. The broken mirror of
shattered identity. The shipwreck of memory in the waters
of the wash-houses. The shifting sands. The indestructible
waterweeds. The moaning of the stones. The echo of the
walls. The laughter of the ravens.

She's no longer here. She lives in the city of the dead.
The ditch. The charnel house. The regestation of common
bones in the womb of the earth. She's no longer here.
She's with us. She's the dust of our footsteps. Her foetal
body nourishes the trees. She lives high on the hill. The
common dwelling-place. The womb of the world. She
runs among the reeds. She brings forth her young in the
nests of birds. She jumps over the dams in mountain
streams. She puts our crown of chestnut leaves together.
She weaves our fern-leaf clothing. Don't be afraid. She
lives in the bowels of the earth. The depths of our flesh.
Molecules they know nothing about. Red acids they want
to cure. In our brains she lives in everything they want to
destroy. The memory inscribed in our flesh. The refusal to
separate. A common identity. Alike and different. The
reuniting of opposites. The unknowable. The name of the

unnameable. The unpronounceable sound between one and someone.

They say she's no longer there. It's up to me to take her place. There must always be one woman. The smallest. The weakest. The most fragile. There must always be one in each generation. At each new beginning. There must always be one to protect them. There must always be one to be an emissary. There must always be one to join things together again.

Do you hear the blue barque of the ferryman? I'm the one he's coming to fetch. Do you hear him? Don't be afraid. It's the song of the glaciers. The thirty-thousand year-old woman is sleeping in our arms. Don't be afraid. She's asleep. She's the mother of us all.

She has kept the meaning. The consent. The memory of origins. The stones and mountains. The cliffs and volcanoes. The harvests and fields. The flocks crossing the horizon. The fruit of the gardens. The alliance with the earth. The alliance of the part and the whole. The sense of the world. Its memory. The marshlands. The serpents rising up toward the land. The great birds and fish. The origins.

Two times one: one. The emergence of thought. The tool in the hand. The cut stone. Polished stone. Melted metals. Matter transformed. The beginning of separation. The rupture. The murderer disrupting the order of things. Domination. Possession. Separation. Two times two: two.

The meaning of the world. The memory of beginnings. The same for everyone. The cave of the womb. The mother suffocating the foetus. The mother rejecting the foetus. The mother drying up the foetus. But the foetus defends itself. The foetus secretes its own survival. The foetus paralyses rejection. The balancing of opposites. The knowledge of death. Two times one: one.

Memory the same for everyone. The knowledge of death in the mother's belly. The order of the world. The order of things. The order of opposites. The origins of thought in the memory of death. The origin. How can one conceive it save in conception? Two times one: one. The original garden. The womb of the world. The gestation of the species. The digestance. The tombs. The dolmens. The pyramids. The dead becoming digested foetuses again. The raised menhirs replacing the living in perpetuity. A love song. The sense of things. The sense of words. The sense of the world. The memory of unity.

They destroy our brains because they can't bear not being able to separate. They inhabit the earth from before. The earth of total reason. The earth of union and separation. The earth of the union of opposites and negation. The earth of chaos. The earth of the womb. The earth of knowledge and life. They destroy our brains because they can't put up with difference. We guard in us that half of reason from which they have excluded themselves. We guard the philosopher's stone that they can't excise. We haven't left the original garden. We live in all the cards of the deck. They have it in their hands. But they use it to question the future. They corrupt it. Because they can't keep from dominating. They can't write themselves into the world. They can't live the writing. They have the game in their hands but they don't know how to read it.

They're knowledgeable. Very knowledgeable. Too knowledgeable. They know drugs. They cure the red acids, but they don't know about the seventh day. They name the illnesses they invent but don't know the fire that dries up knowledge. They're knowledgeable. Very knowledgeable. Too knowledgeable. They know how to cut up our brains, but can't put the two halves of reason back together.

They laugh at us, the normal. The healthy. The reasonable. They lock us up. Cure us. Separate us. One day they will tear out my brain. For the autopsy. For the demonstration. The reassuration. For the peace of mind of all the non-living. Grouped one against the other. So no one can get out of the chains. All these normal ones. These reasonable ones. Refusing to live for fear of suffering. Renouncing love for the fear of asking. Renouncing the search for the fear of walking.

My brain torn out because of all these hands outstretched. All these hands that reach beyond the shifting sands of language. All these hands that reach beyond the silt of my despair. All these hands that horrify them by discovering the charnel houses they have created. My brain torn out in their dissecting tray. In their glass of formol. On their laboratory bench. My brain with its flowers and crevices. Its ravines and mountains. Its cherries and fields. And I'll cry out again. I'll shout out their neglect. Their resigning. Their lies. I'll cry out that they have sold themselves. They won't be able to make me keep quiet. They'll put on rubber gloves. But my brain will still get their hands wet. They won't be able to touch it. Nor my marshland body. Nor my river life. They come from a continent they have lost.

The hour of death and rebirth has come. Reason emerging from unreason. The reunion of the murderer and the murdered. They are one and the same. The murderer is going to find his land. The murdered one is going to be reunited. The hour has come to think together fusion and separation. State of being and action. The imaginary and the real. The hour has come to return to the original garden. The road is not barred. We are the ones who forbid it to ourselves. The hour has come to eat the fruit of the tree of life also. It grows in the garden of the cerebellum. And it makes us like the spirit.

To be nothing any longer but a cry. The screaming of fractured light. The witness of the world's devastated body. The memory of meaning. Being nothing anymore but a body torn apart. Nothing but suffering suffering. The suffering of hanging on. The suffering of not being able to deviate. The suffering of not being able to capitulate.

You say suffering is useless. But it isn't. It serves to make you cry out. To warn of the senselessness. To warn of the disorder. To warn of the world's fracture. You say that suffering is useless. But it isn't. It serves as a witness to the broken body.

I'm dying of despair. I'm dying of their lie. I'm dying of their conformity to any mould whatsoever as long as it reassures them. As long as it dispenses them from thinking. As long as it dispenses them from living. I'm dying from this oozing of words. I'm dying of their meaning. I'm dying of writing. Of trees by the river bank. Of insects on the stones. Of meadows and marshlands. Of the screaming of willows. Of the tinkling of oats. Of the cry of poppies. I'm dying of the breathing of things. Of the breath of the world through my body. Of the inspiration and the expiration.

It's nothing. It's the blue barque of the ferryman. The last journey. The one before the first. The one time only journey. The first time journey. The barque of the ferryman ferrying my burial. The blue barque carrying my body and my defoliated reason away, the meeting again with the earth. The second to last card. The end of the path. The last Arcana.

So much water is needed to get across. All the water from the fountains. All the water from tears. All the water from the wash-houses. It's the place beyond suffering. The unique journey. The one time only journey. The river without banks. The blue barque of the ferryman bearing my burial.

The ladybirds walk in front because of the colour of blood. Next come the flies that I loved so much as companions. Next come the flies for having shared my meals. Next come the wasps for having killed so many without looking for the nest. Next come the flies and the wasps for having killed each other. Next comes the coffin borne by ants. There are so many that each one is useless. There are so many that each one is unique. There are so many that each one is superfluous. Next comes the coffin borne by ants because it is from them that I learned to love life. It's from them that I learned the love of the murderer. It's from them that I learned about the other half of the world. It's from them that I learned the land of whole reason. The lizard walks alongside. The lizard has a big hat. He announces the news. He announces the time of the separation. He announces the time of living. He announces the time of the murderers. The lizard walks alongside. He holds my hand. The lizard walks alongside because he was my love. The frogs follow beating their drums. The frogs follow a cortège of mourners. The frogs follow with their white handkerchiefs. The frogs follow sobbing because they are my friends. Next come the June bugs, they were my comrades. We played together in the time of the sweet chestnut-trees. We played together for love of periwinkles. Next come the June bugs, my comrades when the soil was being ploughed. Next comes the scorpion ending the procession. The tragic and solitary scorpion. The scorpion of silence and venom. He was my brother.

The deaths of the brain, I know of seven. But the death of the world I won't be able to know. For it goes on. It goes on in the memory of our cells. In the cry of the tortured earth. In the waiting of the wheat begging for rain. In the offered river hollowing out its bed. In my flesh weeping in the depths of the crematorium. In the waterweed flooding the funeral pyre. In the drowned body resisting the brazier.

They burn me but I don't die. I am living from the impossible death of the World. I'm living from the murder of the murderer. I'm living from the bruise of the bruised. I'm living from the stone that unites them. I'm living from everything they deny but can't destroy. The laughter of the birds in the fields. The hissing of the serpent in the ravine. The love of our knowing bodies.

I'm living from my love of opposites and negation. Of fusion and separation. Of my body for bodies. Of my body for the earth. Of my body for life. I'm living from the memory they have lost. From the knowledge they refuse. The waterweeds they reject. The wash-houses they abandon.

I live from the death they constantly throw in my face. I'm the last card in the game. The one that has a name and no place. The one that ends the game and begins it over again. The Fool they can't checkmate.

I will go off to die in the country of the living bearing in my torn flesh the only goods they have left me. The songs. The love of François. And above all, the flight of the ravens.